# CLANCY of the UNDERTOW

## CHRISTOPHER CURRIE

TEXT PUBLISHING MELBOURNE AUSTRALIA

textpublishing.com.au

The Text Publishing Company
Swann House
22 William Street
Melbourne Victoria 3000
Australia

First published in 2016 by The Text Publishing Company

Cover and page design by Imogen Stubbs
Cover photograph by Miquel Llonch / Stocksy
Typeset in Sabon 11/16 by J & M Typesetting

Printed in Australia by Griffin Press, an Accredited ISO AS/NZS 14001:2004 Environmental Management System printer

National Library of Australia Cataloguing-in-Publication entry
Creator: Currie, Christopher, author.
Title: Clancy of the undertow / by Christopher Currie.
ISBN: 9781925240405 (paperback)
9781922253194 (ebook)
Target Audience: For young adults.
Subjects: Love stories.
Dewey Number: A823.4

# CLANCY OF THE UNDERTOW

Christopher Currie is a Brisbane writer. His first book, a novel for adults called *The Ottoman Motel*, was shortlisted for the Commonwealth Book Prize and the Queensland Literary Awards in 2012. *Clancy of the Undertow* is his first YA novel.

furioushorses.com
@furioushorses
facebook.com/christophercurrieauthor

For Roy Fox, who taught me the power of curiosity,
the benefit of patience and the importance of empathy.

She's got this nearly chinless face, which isn't as bad as it sounds because she's European and her nose bends over in a poetic way. And she's small, birdy, gorgeous. She dresses in silk blouses the colour and texture of cream. Pencil skirts that have an actually pencil shape: that sort of perfect thing.

Eloise and me. She's thirty-two, voluptuous, perfect. I am sixteen, with the physique of a tree frog.

This is the two of us, our top halves poking out above the makeup counter. Our island in a shopping-centre sea. Usually, we're both here only on a Saturday; the other six days we split. During the holidays I'm Mondays, Tuesdays and Thursdays and on these days, pretty much nothing gets sold. For some reason this is okay. I spend my time giving people directions to other shops, and the rest of it perfecting doodles and playlists in the notebook which is supposed to be for the takings and customer orders.

It's better than school, but only because of the air-conditioning. Eloise is the only reason I stay here, that I put up with the days of boredom and humiliation in this retail prison.

Eloise is the only reason anyone comes to the booth—or rather, the Beauty Station. She purrs and preens over the country women who waddle up from the International Carvery to have their gravy-stained faces primped and poked by this mysterious European queen. And they all leave with the Full Beauty Package (*not that you need it darling, but the men, eh? They want a little colour to your cheeks...*) which will require replenishment in just under a month's time. Every Saturday we make the week's takings in the three hours everyone in town turns up to buy the family groceries.

It's late afternoon now, Thursday. Eloise has come in to check inventory when she knows it will be quiet. The shoppers are all but gone and it's back to the head-crushing tedium. The only thing keeping me going is my afternoon visit from Reeve. Today he ambles up in his dark blue uniform about three-thirty. He has in his hand something that purports to be a juice, but whose colour would seem to place it outside the plant kingdom.

'What's the two-oh-three?' I say to him.

'It's all on the down,' he says. 'Nuthin' but goddam happers, whackin' out and fliptoppin'.'

I nod knowledgeably. 'Streets be a jungle, yo.'

Reeve takes a sip of his drink, closing his eyes as he

2

takes in the sugar. His face can only devote itself to one activity at a time. After he swallows, he laughs. 'How's business, ladies?'

Eloise folds a handtowel and nods. 'Security Guard Lewis,' she says. 'How are you?'

Reeve nods back. 'Very well, thank you.' We're never sure when Eloise is joking.

'Anything we can help you with today?' I say. 'I could offer you a lovely foundation to set your complexion off against your uniform. What colour would you call your shirt?'

'Ocean of despair.'

I snort. Eloise clears her throat beside me. She has banter tolerance of exactly one minute.

'Better get back to it,' I say. 'Time waits for no tan.'

Reeve groans. 'Awful, Clancy. Just awful. What time you closing up today?'

'Darling,' says Eloise, 'I feel there will be more sales before the day is out.' She flutters a hand up against her face.

'Five-thirty then,' I say, trying to hide my tone of resignation.

'All right,' says Reeve, 'well I might see you once more, crime waves permitting.' He gives us a lazy salute and strolls off.

When Reeve is out of earshot, Eloise leans over to me. 'He is quite something, that boy.'

I cluck my tongue. 'He's *something*.'

3

'Ah, to be young again, Clancy!' Eloise claps her hands together, swooning.

'Jeez,' I say, feeling my neck flush red because it clearly hates me. 'He's just a friend.'

'Ah, well, it is better to have lost in love than ever more.'

'Right. Yep.' I duck behind the counter to look in a drawer that has suddenly caught my attention. I still can't decide whether Eloise actually doesn't know the real words to proverbs, or whether this is an aspect of the character she plays.

'You just have to believe in yourself,' she says. I feel something in my hair before I realise she's stroking it. I jump, which is not easy when you're crouching, and then try to move myself away from her. My duck-waddle fails and I topple to the floor. I observe the complex ecosystem of dust and used cotton balls under the counter.

'Are you all right, darling?'

'Absolutely,' I say. 'Completely in my element.'

*The afternoon passes,* with no more customers, and I leave just after five. I change into my boots and hurry out of the shopping centre before Reeve can find me and we have to have a real conversation, without the social safety barrier of a large white counter between us.

Coming down the escalators the knife guy is there at his display table and he winks at me, his hand resting on the hilt of a dagger shaped like a dragon's head. For the umpteenth time, I realise I could just reach down off the escalator and pick up a blade and make the news. Not that I ever would, but sometimes I think it, just for the stupid thrill.

I leave through the big sliding doors and the afternoon humidity drapes itself across my face. I've just rubbed off the worst of the makeup in the shopping centre bathroom, leaving on what I hope is the right amount. Eloise has taught me how to apply makeup, but only in a way that suits her strong features. On my nondescript face, the dark eye shadow and dramatic slash of lipstick just makes me look like something from a straight-to-DVD horror franchise.

My bike is there on the rack, still somehow not stolen even though I leave the lock conspicuously undone. Dad refuses to buy me a new bike until this one 'wears out' and so as usual I hop on my too-small red BMX, *Lightning Lady* written in huge pearlescent letters on the frame, and pedal out of the carpark. I often consider riding it out of town and abandoning it, but I'm a terrible liar and Dad would be able to tell and then I'd have no bike.

My stupid backpack keeps hitching up my shirt so I spend most of the ride holding it down until eventually I sling the backpack over the handlebars, and then it's hard to steer and so I have to go really slow and I can feel the drivers of the cars buzzing past judging me but that's just the way my life is. I turn off the main road and shudder over the unsealed path that runs beside the river. I pull up next to the play equipment and fling my bike into the dirt, hoping to encourage an irreparable crack in the chassis. No such luck.

Soon I'm sitting behind the skate park, with its stench of dust and petrol, pretending to read a book. All the guys are pretty much just silhouettes against the sky. One by one, they teeter on the lip of the ramp and drop away, their shape replaced by sound. The hum of wheels on concrete. The rest of them are huddled on the other side, making fume-tents with their shirts or smoking or both. It stinks here. There is, however, no better place to watch the vacant lot across the fence where the cars are gathering.

They're parked at mad angles, a protest to symmetry. More join every minute, appearing first as dirty clouds from behind the hill, then swinging into focus with carefully choreographed fishtails that send up even more dust. The crowd cheers each time a new car arrives. Everyone coming in from work. Or not-work.

Thursday is Student Night in Barwen. Named after the chalkboard claim the Criterion never takes down from outside its entrance. It's sort of a Barwen in-joke, because no one here really *studies*, not in the sense Student Night usually means. A few adult learners at the TAFE, probably, but that's it. Still, tradition is tradition, and Thursday night means party night.

Finally, the car I'm waiting for arrives, and it gets the biggest cheer. A mustard-brown Monaro, flashing its lights. Buggs gets out, unfolding his body from his modified drivers seat that's positioned impossibly low to the floor. This always struck me as stupid, because the sun visor wouldn't keep the sun out of his eyes, but Buggs isn't known as someone who things through. He takes off his cap, smooths his hair, puts the cap back on. Predictable as hell. He kneads his lips, fishing in his pocket for cigarettes, striding over to a group of guys by the half-pipe. I keep my eyes on the car.

The tiny car light flicks on and my heart jags because she's there, painting Cleopatra edges to her eyes, peering

7

at the rearview mirror. Sasha Strickland, leaning back to shuffle on a jeans leg, kicking one foot out at the evening air. All the guys have gone with Buggs to the edge of the skate ramp. Nobody looking at Sasha except for me. Nobody sees the three holes in her stockings that look like a ghost's face. I think of being a ghost, of being invisible. Being in the back seat as Sasha prepares for a night out. Leaning my ghost head close to her cheek and feeling its heat.

I realise I've got my hands down the sides of my boots where the elastic has wafered. I need new shoes. I'll never impress anyone with old boots and old clothes and an old bike. I glance at my watch but already know I have to leave. Sasha gets out of the car and stretches sort of the way a cat stretches, every muscle shivering out. She's cut her hair since last week, framing her face with straight edges. Someone said she goes to Brisbane to get it done. Most local girls go to Classic Cuts or Real Beauty, which are basically the same place because any girl who goes in there comes out with identical skanky highlights and claw-nails and eyelashes like a giraffe. They're all fake tanned, too, but not Sasha. She's pale. Whenever you see that crowd together, smoking outside the Cri or by the council building or outside Macca's on the weekend, Sasha always stands out, like a vampire in a wheatfield. Black hair, black jeans. She's with Buggs, but only because it makes them a crazy famous couple.

Buggs is from a family that's been here since the town

was settled and his uncle used to be the mayor and half the town is run by his other uncles and cousins. His last name is Pfister, which is hilarious, but no one's allowed to make fun of him because of who his family is even though his first name is actually Barnaby, a fact that made me laugh for five straight minutes when I found out. Buggs is a massive douche. He works in his dad's auto shop, but he's never really there. He spends most of his time tinkering with his own car, or sitting at the front bar of the Cri. He's super thin and stooped over, and his nose is almost flat to his face, but he's somehow the coolest guy in town, which is why Sasha is with him. Must be.

All the guys are laughing by the half-pipe and I hear cans opening and bottle caps flipping off and I get up and leave before anyone sees me. I take one look back and Sasha's leaning against Buggs like he's a useful tree, smoking and staring off into her own middle distance, her transformation complete. Daytime travel agent to night-time smalltown royalty. I dig my nails into my palm and stifle a huge, self-pitying sigh. She'll never notice me. I'll never even be a small part of her world.

*I cycle back* up the dirt path, not bothering to get up off my seat as I judder across the tiny stones. What's the point? I pedal furiously up the hill and cut in behind CityView Motel's carpark. Throw my bike over the fence and drag it up the cow paddock. As always, I can't tell what's a divot and what's a cowpat but I plough on regardless. There's a crowd of cockatoos dotting the grass white and they flap madly as I walk through them, flying up as a big swarm, circling one of the two huge eucalypts on each side of our house. Late summer is brimful with birdscreech until even after dark. Titch is there by the front steps standing in a puddle of water he's made by letting the hose run.

'Turn that off,' I say.

'Mum said I could.' He has on one of his stupid skater caps, decorated with skulls.

'You're wasting water.'

'There's no restrictions,' he says. 'La Niña is in full effect.'

Titch is turning into such a smart-arse. Where once stood my fun little brother now stands the chrysalis of a bogan butterfly. 'Dad home?'

'Yeah, but he's steaming.'

Great. *Steaming* means Dad's had a bad day and he isn't happy about it.

A little while ago, middle of winter, just after Dad'd come off compo and was doing traffic work, he came home and we were out front chopping wood and when he got out of the car we started laughing because his sweat turned into steam and it looked like his head had been on fire. He swore at us something chronic. Since then, a *steaming* Dad is not a good thing.

'That's perfect,' I say. Dad in a bad mood means Mum in a bad mood, meaning I can't be in the least bit fed up with my stupid boring life without getting a long lecture on the inherent value of something.

Titch sinks further into the mud and I hope to God he keeps sinking.

Inside the house I can already feel the tension. Dad's fluoro workshirt is hanging on the chair, a smear of jam on the breast pocket. I can picture him flinging it off before disappearing for a long shower—more steam from under the bathroom door.

'Clancy.' Mum's standing by the sink, new rubber gloves nearly glowing green.

'Hi,' I say. 'What's going on?'

Mum makes that face where her cheeks pinch up

11

towards her eyes: to a stranger, a smile. 'I need you to go and get your brother.'

'Titch is out the front. I'm not cleaning him up though.'

'Angus. I need you to get Angus.'

'Why?' My older brother is living at home *temporarily*, which means—knowing Angus—probably forever. The rule is he has to make his own dinner unless he tells Mum otherwise. He hardly ever does. Stays out late just about every night.

'Can you just go and get him?' Mum's cheeks have flushed, twin comets against her skin.

'What's going on?' I say it more serious this time, in the voice I use when I'm trying to make sense of people. My feet are already aching in my boots. The last thing I want is to cycle across town looking for my dropkick brother.

Mum turns back to the sink. 'Just do it, Clancy. It's important.'

'Jesus. Can you just make him buy a phone?'

Mum throws up her hands, as if this means something.

'How'm I supposed to know where he is?' I say. 'I have to go out on my bike in the dark?'

'You know where he'll be. He can drive you back.' The tone in Mum's voice is heavy and weird.

I perform an offended pirouette and tramp back out of the house. I've tried words with my parents. Now I just use silence.

*I clip on* my front light and coast back down the hill. I'm always the one who has to do the responsible stuff. Titch is too young and Angus is too unreliable. Still a year before I can drive and I'm the only person in our family responsible for getting things done. Dad works weird hours now he's on the road crew and Mum hardly leaves the house if she doesn't get any teaching work. Still, Mum's right—there's no doubt where Angus is at this time of night. Up the top of the observatory, drinking, smoking pot and planning the next stage of his severely unambitious life.

I pedal hard down through town and out past Red Rooster and KFC. When the streetlights stop I switch on the weak front light and close my eyes down the hills. Angus'll pay for me having to do this. On top of whatever ragging Dad's going to give him. He probably parked Dad in last night or used up the shampoo or ate the last of the salt and vinegar chips—any number of things Dad would want to haul him into line for. Dad's job means he gets to stand still for hours at a time in the middle of nowhere, stewing over the smallest things us kids have done wrong. Especially Angus, who in Dad's eyes is constantly wasting his time. Which is, basically, entirely accurate.

Six months ago Angus quit uni. He came home two weeks into his course complaining that his teachers were *biased*. I told him they were probably biased towards people who actually did work, and he moped about that for days as if I hadn't just pointed out a basic true fact. Now when he isn't on the couch at home he's out wasting his savings at the Cri or various dipshit gathering points around town, concocting intricate schemes that won't work. He disappears overnight sometimes, doing God knows what.

I tap the brakes when I see the pilot light up ahead and coast to a stop at the bottom of the observatory. Despite its name, it's basically just a steel tower with a platform on top, a set of metal steps going up four storeys on the side of the highway. It has some sort of scientific significance, like, where it's placed you can see certain stars or something, but no one ever goes up there for anything to do with astronomy.

I ring my bike's bell at what I hope is an annoying volume and shout up, 'Angus you gotta come home!' and I can see him up there, the lit tip of a joint hanging in the air.

He doesn't say anything so I get off my bike and kick

the base of the metal stairwell. 'You gotta drive me home! Mum made me come out here to get you cause Dad's steaming!' I hear him laughing. 'Angus!' I shout again. 'Can you finish jerking off and get down here?'

I hear the clang of feet on the steps. 'Jesus,' he shouts. 'Queen of comedy.'

'Hurry up.'

He slides down the last set of stairs like a sailor on a submarine. 'What's happened?' he says. His hair's all messed up by the wind and he's wearing one of his disgusting tank tops from Dollars and Sense that says *Fat Kids Are Harder to Kidnap*.

I shrug my shoulders. 'Mum just says you have to come home.'

Angus rubs his hands together. 'I'm kind of busy.'

'With what?'

'Planning the Big Hunt.'

I give him a look, like *that again?*

'Whatever,' I say. 'I'm hungry. Dad'll probably just give us a talk about hanging the toilet paper the right way round and we can all get on with our lives.'

Angus shakes his head. 'This family,' he says, with the world-weary tone of someone who has never had to take responsibility for anything his entire life.

My bike's bouncing around in the tray of Angus's ute because he hasn't got any rope and I keep looking back, expecting it to fly off onto the road at any moment.

'It's fine,' he says. 'Don't you understand basic physics?'

'Like you do.'

Angus is chewing on like eight sticks of gum. They're wadded up in his cheek and he probably thinks it's cool because it looks like tobacco or something. 'How was work?' he says.

'Okay.'

Angus bats his eyelids. 'Venn are you goink to be keeping zee lipstick on darlink? You are zo attractiff!' I laugh, despite not wanting to. Angus smirks. 'Is Dad actually steaming or is Mum just playing happy families?'

'Dunno. Didn't see him when I got home. Mum looked pretty upset though.'

'Right. Let's hope it's over quickly, then.'

'Gotta get back to the tower? Polish your telescope?'

'Piss off.'

'I hear Pluto's right up in Uranus.'

Angus sighs. 'You think I'm just wasting my time, don't you?'

'What else would you call it?'

'Re-evaluating.'

I put my feet up on the dashboard, which I know he hates. 'Failing, more like.'

'Give us a break, Clance. I've got my whole life to work out what I want to do. I'm planning something pretty important.'

'Chasing made-up monsters.'

'As if. I've done the research. Just have to put it into action.'

'And this is your big plan.'

'You won't be laughing when I'm on the news.'

I don't dignify this with a response. Every few years some drunk spots a cow in the hills outside of town and says he's seen a giant cat. Back in the seventies was when it all started, according to Dad. Some blurry photograph of what was probably a big rock got everyone obsessed with what the paper called the Beast of Barwen. People went out on weekends to try and photograph it or trap it but of course came back empty-handed. Angus has been obsessed with it since coming back home, spending hours on the computer at the library looking at psycho conspiracy sites.

The thing is, he used to love nature: in a proper, real

17

way. He was top of his class in biology—needless to say the only class he was *any* good in; used to watch David Attenborough docos over and over the way other kids watch cartoons. He was the reason I started going to Nature Club. I joined back when I actually admired my brother, but my interest coincided with Angus activating his inevitable male douchebag chromosome and reclassifying anything to do with science as *nerdy shit*.

I still go to Nature Club, but Angus's interests have morphed into making money and finding 'the truth', two vague philo-sophies melded together by various dodgy internet forums and the modern male obsession with Going to the Mines to Earn Easy Dollars.

We drive in silence until we reach the centre of town, where Angus is obliged by some unspoken idiot rule to wind down the windows and cruise slowly up Aggery St. There's a small crowd spilling outside the Cri. I see Buggs's broken head but Sasha's nowhere to be seen.

Suddenly one of them points at Angus's car and shouts out, 'Hey, dickhead!' and Angus grins but then Buggs gives him the finger and the rest of them follow suit.

'Step out the car!' Buggs shouts, walking towards us. Angus slows down but he seems to realise the same time as me that the crowd isn't ragging on him in a friendly way.

One of them goes, 'Hey dickhead, you wanna watch the road!' and another one goes, 'Y'old man oughtta watch the fucken road!' and they're coming right at us and I hit

Angus's leg so he plants his foot and we lurch forward. As we speed away I hear a scraping sound and when I look back I see the front wheel of my bike disappearing over the side of the ute's tray.

Angus is driving fast and shaking his head like he's just seen a puzzle he can't work out. He hoons up the hill too fast and when we come down the driveway Mum's out on the verandah with a torch that's useless because the lights are on anyway. When she sees the car she motions us towards the house.

'The hell's going on?' says Angus.

Mum comes right up to the window. 'Get inside,' she says. 'Both of you. Right now.'

We get out and she pulls us in with one hand on each of our wrists and doesn't say anything when I tell her about my bike. We go through the door and into the empty lounge room.

'Seriously, Mum. What's the deal?' Angus puts his hands on his hips, unintentionally mimicking Dad's default pose.

Mum looks suddenly shaken. 'Just...are you both okay?'

'Yeah,' I say. 'We're fine.'

I wonder if Mum knew about my bike already, but how could she?

'Can you both sit down?'

'Where's Titch?'

'He's in bed. He...Can you kids sit down please? *Now*.'

Mum's put on her forceful teacher's voice, pretending we're both in primary school, which I normally hate, but this time I just do what she says.

Angus sits down next to me and says, quietly, 'What's going on?' and it's weird to hear him talking to Mum without his usual pissy tone.

'Nothing,' she says. 'Nothing.'

And of course neither of us believes her.

We sit there in silence for a while, which is nothing unusual for our family except normally we're saved by the blare of the TV. Mum keeps playing with her hands, checking her fingernails like they hold all the secrets of the universe.

'We were driving home,' I say eventually. 'Some of those dropkicks outside the Cri, some of them were shouting at us. I didn't hear what it was.'

'Something about Dad,' Angus says.

Mum goes, 'Right. I see.'

'Those dickheads are always shouting though.'

'Language!' Mum snaps.

'Where's Dad?' I say. Something like dread shivers down my back. 'Has something happened to him?'

There's a flicker in Mum's face, a rift in the mask of composure. 'He's fine,' she says. 'He's fine.'

Angus leans forward. 'Where is he?'

'Out in the shed. He's fine.'

I sigh. 'Seriously, Mum. What the hell?'

I know something's really up when she doesn't pull me

up for swearing. 'Everything's fine,' she says, hoisting up her fake smile. 'I'm sorry I snapped.'

I stare at her. The amount of time we all spend not talking to each other, it's insane.

I say, 'You made me ride all the way out to get Angus just because of *nothing*. You get us into the house and get us to sit here like a bomb's about to go off, and you won't tell us why.'

'I'm sorry,' she says. She goes to stand up. 'I'd better get—'

'I lost my bike,' I say. 'Because of you, I lost my bike.'

Mum sighs. 'I just don't have time tonight, Clancy.'

'What?'

'Not everything's about you,' she says. 'You and that bike.' She shakes her head and stands up.

'The hell with this,' says Angus. 'Thanks for wasting my time.'

This is when Mum would usually explode. Instead, she just walks out of the room.

*There are containers* of frozen soup in the sink so I take one out and microwave it and eat it watching TV. Everyone's in a different room, as per usual. I can't really concentrate. I keep wanting to hear the shed door roll up, the back door swing back and slam and Dad's footsteps come clomping in. Eventually, I realise this isn't going to happen so I wash up my bowl and spoon and open the fridge and take a swig of milk straight from the container. I smack my lips, but there's no one around to hear it. Just me, the blare of a bad sitcom, the aftertaste of watered-down dinner.

I know tonight means another day petering out without resolution. Our family, basically, is like a bad sitcom. Reality resets. *Join us tomorrow for another madcap adventure of simmering tension and broken dreams! Only on* The Underhills*!* Sometimes I think the only thing holding us together is the fact we all share the same last name, as if we're just in it for the letterhead.

When Angus went off to uni it was a bit different. Mum thought it was maybe a fresh start, so she tried to make us eat together at the table each night, like a *real family*. It disintegrated pretty quickly, though. Dad's weird work hours meant he wasn't there half the time, and Titch's feral-pig eating style was nearly impossible to put up with. Which left just me and Mum; the worst possible scenario. She'd think it was Serious Bonding Time and start to use phrases like 'just us girls' and 'a really nice chat', an obvious lead-up to questions about sex or my period or drugs (no, yes, yes) like we were best friends.

There's no way in the known universe I will ever be friends with my mother. I know girls who have Mum Best Friends. I see them every Saturday morning at the shopping centre. Matching tans, matching hair, matching T-shirts that spell out, in sequins, DRAMA QUEEN or ZERO TO BITCH IN 2.5 DRINKS. Skankle-Dee and Cankle-Dum.

Whenever we'd eat together, Mum would always lean forward with her fingers steepled, like *I wish to broach a subject with you, Clancy*, as if we were in the United Nations ('Now, Estonia, I know other countries your age smoke marijuana, and it's fine to experiment, but I want you to know the dangers…').

So we went back to kind of normal—dinner whenever, in front of the TV—but then Angus came back from uni and him and Dad went at it harder than ever, Dad thinking Angus had failed, Angus thinking Dad was being too hard

23

on him. I feel for my brother, really, because I know he wants to do better, but at the same time he's such a shit-head and makes such shithead decisions.

I lock the front door and go upstairs. I see light under Angus's door and stop outside it for a moment. I want to knock. I want to know what he thinks about what happened tonight. I want him, actually, to reassure me it'll all blow over and be fine by the morning. I stare at the old *X-Files* poster on his door, telling me The Truth is Out There, hanging above a picture of a nuclear preparation pamphlet he cut out of his Study of Society textbook. You can still see the Ninja Turtle puffy stickers around the doorknob, stuck so fast that Angus couldn't prise them off and had to paint over them.

The door suddenly swings open. 'Whaddya doing?' Angus says. 'Trying to listen in?'

'No,' I say, sounding suddenly guilty of doing exactly that. 'But you should probably put your tinfoil helmet on in case the government is recording this conversation.'

'I never did that.'

'I saw you wearing it.'

'Piss off.'

I have a sudden thought. 'Can you drop me at Landsdowne tomorrow morning?'

'Nerd Club? Isn't that just weekends?'

'School holidays, genius.'

'Get Mum to do it.'

'Don't think she'll be in the mood.'

'No way. That old pedo'll try and talk to me.'

'Just drop me off.'

'It's fine for you. Mister P doesn't get hard for little girls.'

'Get over yourself, Spangus.'

*Mister P* was George Parry, a scientist who'd worked at the Research Station for as long as anyone could remember. He's run Nature Club forever, never been paid, put up with ungrateful turds like Angus for years. He *is* a weird guy, but really nice. Just because he doesn't have a girlfriend or a wife people have always said he was up to something sinister, but he's just devoted to his job. Passionate about passing on a love of nature. To be fair, though, he does look quite a lot like a pedo.

'He always tries to get me to come back,' Angus says. 'Like I'd want to hang out with a bunch of little wieners counting grass stalks.' He puts his hand over his mouth, pretending he's said the wrong thing. 'No offence.'

'Dickhead.' Nature Club is one of the few things in life I actually enjoy, and he knows it.

Angus reaches behind the door and lifts out his backpack.

'Where are you going?'

'Getting out of this nuthouse.'

'For good?' My voice cracks. I have this thing where I sound like a Disney princess sometimes and I hate it.

'I'm just going out.' He goes to push past me.

'What do you reckon's up with Dad?' I say, blocking his way.

'No idea,' he says. 'Probably buggered up another job.'

'I'm sure it's nothing, though. Right?'

Angus shoulders me out of the way. 'Piss off, Pantsy.'

'What about my bike?' I say, hanging onto him the way I used to when I was little. Making him drag me along. 'Why do you think Buggs and that were yelling at us?'

'The hell should I know?' Angus shakes free of my grip and tramps down the stairs, giving me the finger over his shoulder.

My mouth feels furry all of a sudden and I can taste the minestrone mixing with the milk in my stomach. There's no light under Mum and Dad's bedroom door and I hope this means Mum hasn't heard us. She's probably listening to the radio anyway, curled up on one side of the enormous bed that belonged to her mum. The bed she's so often told me will one day be passed down to me, and I tell her there's no way I'm going to sleep in a bed that two generations of my family have had sex on.

I go into my room and perform my patented kick-the-door-closed-and-face-plant-onto-my-doona manoeuvre. It's how I end most days, and I stay there, nose pressed into the salmon-coloured acrylic, for as long as it takes to forget the day I've just had. Tonight, I stay there for probably twenty minutes. Before long my face starts to tingle from either too much or too little blood flow, but I stay there until I can make some sort of sense of what's happened in the past few hours.

Dad probably *did* bugger something up. He's on thin ice with the council as it is. After his back went they really wanted to fire him; instead they stuck him out in the middle of nowhere on roadwork crews. Traffic duties. In pain most of the time, probably. I heard him talking to Mum about it. Night crews were incompetent, he said. Got bugger all done, just stood around big machines drinking spiked coffee while he stood a couple of hundred metres up the road with a STOP/SLOW sign to spin.

How the hell am I supposed to get to Nature Club tomorrow? No bike, no Angus, no Mum. I could drive, but Dad never lets me practise. I have to wait nearly half a year to even sit the learners test, which is ridiculous. Angus drove when he was sixteen, and there's pictures of Dad on *his* dad's property driving a tractor when he couldn't even see over the steering wheel. Plus, Dad used to be in a motorcycle gang—Angus got him to admit it one night after a couple of beers—so he doesn't have a leg to stand on. I'll just have to ask again tomorrow, or at least threaten to take the car keys until my demands are met.

God. Another day. Same as this one.

I finally push myself up off the bed when I can't actually feel my face, and get a headspin when I stand up. I stare at myself in the mirror and notice a purple tinge beneath my eyes. Lying on the bed has pushed my hair up on one side so it looks like I have an even more wonky oblong head. Just one of my many fun physical faults. I get

27

my towel from the hook behind the door and drape it over the mirror so I can get into my pyjamas without having to accidentally catch a glimpse of myself in my underwear.

I climb into bed and I've just got comfy when I realise I haven't brushed my teeth, closed my door or turned out the light.

Every. Damn. Time.

*The next morning,* as predicted, Mum's pretending like nothing's wrong. She knocks on my door at some insane hour and says 'Brekkie's up!' in her primary-teacher-happy-storytime voice. I know instantly what sort of morning we're in for. Mum's rubber band of stress has snapped and she's back to Happy Housewife.

'Morning, sweetie.' My door opens and Mum's head pokes in. 'Time to get up.'

As usual, my limbs have attempted to achieve cold fusion with my doona and I spend some moments working out which way is up.

'It's getting late, Clancy. Even for the holidays. You want to enjoy the day, don't you?'

'*Want* and *expect* are different things.'

'Toast's about to pop. Got some of that jam you like.'

'Mum.' I raise an arm as a surrender flag. 'I will get up if you promise to take me to Nature Club.'

'That today, is it?'

'Yup.'

'Well, I don't know. I do have some…things to take care of.'

I roll over in bed, finally freeing myself from the doona. 'I won't even bring up my missing bike,' I say. 'I won't ask anything about what happened yesterday.'

Mum looks at me intently, and I wonder if I've crossed a line.

'Be ready to leave at nine-thirty,' she says. I've chosen my bargain wisely.

My body, trained to move nowhere except deeper into my bedding, refuses my brain's orders to get up. I lie there for a few more moments, feeling—I'm pretty sure—like a mountain climber psyching themselves for a final push to the summit. Something's nagging at me, though, beyond my usual tiredness. Thoughts of last night.

My hair's stuck down to my forehead and I realise I've had night sweats again, the first for ages. A deep uneasiness somewhere in my stomach. What *did* happen to Dad last night? Buggs and his mates might be rolled-gold douchebags, but even they must have had a reason to go after Angus and me so hard.

Eventually, somehow, I find myself seated comatose at the breakfast table. Titch is across from me, his face centimetres away from a slurry of neon cereal, hoovering it up with his open mouth. Angus leans against the kitchen counter holding a steaming mug. His new thing is herbal tea, basically thirty bucks' worth of twigs and dirt he ordered from a crackpot 'health' website. He'd told me the tea was meant to 'increase stamina', after which I wanted to know exactly zero per cent more.

Mum's rushing around like we're all running late, which we aren't. She puts a cup of coffee in front of me.

'Where's Dad?' I say.

'Sleeping.' She says it forcefully, the way she does where you can actually hear the full stop at the end. She folds her arms, like *the Mother's decision is final. No correspondence will be entered into.*

And I don't have the energy to challenge her.

Angus throws his mug in the sink and says, 'I'm gorn.'

I go, 'Big day at the sperm bank?' Titch snorts and Angus hits me on the back of the head.

'Clancy, *please*,' says Mum. 'Titch, finish your cereal. Angus, don't speak like a hooligan.' All of a sudden, her harsh tone is absent, and she sounds like she's about to cry.

We all stop and mumble apologies, storing away the retaliations for later.

No one speaks to anyone else until Mum and I are in the car, pulling out of the driveway. Over the crunch of the gravel she says, 'We do a good job, don't we?'

'A good job?' I'm busy synching up my iPod for the drive and I don't really hear her.

'Your dad and I? Our...parenting. It's been okay?'

I sense an impending Deep and Meaningful—a scene from a daytime movie where I'm a slightly faded child

31

star, tears welling in my eyes, going *Are you and Dad... getting a divorce?*

I decide to play it safe. 'Your parenting's been fine. None of us are on hard drugs. Titch isn't pregnant.'

Mum lets a pause fall between us, the exact length of a failed joke. She pulls out onto the main road. 'I just don't want any of you kids to be unhappy. Your dad doesn't either.'

'Yeah, no, it's fine.' Cars are even worse than dinner tables for forced conversation. I start to wonder how much it would actually hurt if I opened the door and threw myself onto the nature strip. But because I'm basically a decent person, I say, 'Is everything, you know, okay?'

Mum stretches her neck, and then her head snaps back into place. 'Oh, fine!' she says, too brightly. 'You know me, always worrying.' She laughs. It's not very convincing. 'Your dad just gets so busy, and I get so stressed out. I just...want you all to know that we love you, no matter what happens.'

I notice Mum's taking the long way to Landsdowne, skirting around the edge of town instead of going straight through it. I don't say anything, busying myself instead with the iPod. Scrolling scrolling scrolling.

We pull up outside the gates just before ten. Faded green writing on the sign: *Landsdowne Research Station*. I feel myself relaxing, muscle by muscle. The whole drive over, Mum's been plying me in a slightly manic tone with the type of lame sayings you'd find on the insides of greeting cards. Being true to yourself, overcoming the odds. I have to ask her again if she's sure everything's okay but she just gives me more platitudes about staying strong and keeping my head held high, like I'm a synchronised swimmer on a losing streak.

She gives me an awkward, too-long kiss on the temple as I try to get out of the car.

'Jeez,' I say. 'You haven't put lipstick on my head, have you?'

'You have a good morning, sweetie. Be true to yourself. Say hi to your friends from me.'

I give her my best salute and escape before she can land another kiss. Then I stand and stare at her until she drives away. She's always asking about my 'friends' at the club, and I know that nothing would deliver her more pleasure—or me more horror—than her ever meeting any of them.

Every time she drops me off, all she wants is for me to invite her through the gates, and there's no way in hell that's ever going to happen.

She drives off and I keep standing there for a minute, enjoying a rare moment of solitude. It's these moments I love the most. Between two worlds, neither in parental care nor under responsible supervision. Not at home or at school or anywhere where I have to be *accounted for*. I love the thrill of this feeling. I love that I'll be away from here soon. Away from Barwen, my family, school, *everything*.

Somehow, even the animal smell outside the gates is relaxing. I peer across the road at the feedlots, empty today and just a jumble of wooden railings and the sweet hint of stale dung. They have these insane livestock auctions out here each month, a whole pack of red-faced farmers in rodeo shirts and bent Akubras stacked in to shout at each other through the dust. I've only been once properly, with Dad when I was younger, when one of his cricket mates wanted to buy some breeding cows.

In those days, Saturday mornings were a negotiation. I'd endure a series of parental chores in exchange for a trip to the newsagents, where I'd buy a comic book or one of those magazines where you'd build a dollhouse or dinosaur skeleton week by week, the first issue being incredibly cheap and the rest of them mind-bogglingly expensive. Dad always started steaming at the price of the second issue so I ended up with a room full of abandoned projects: a single T-Rex rib-bone, a piece of lonely amethyst, a teddy bear's arm.

I turn back and head up to the wonky prefab cabin that serves as the station's reception office. The flyscreen's hanging open but I still knock, like I always do.

'Clancy, yes, good, hello.' George Parry's voice comes from inside the cabin.

My eyes adjust to the dim light inside and he's sitting behind the reception desk, his thin hairy legs crossed underneath. He looks up and he's wearing wraparound Polaroids, even inside. Part of his eternal outfit. He grins and all the bristles of his beard seem to rearrange themselves. Eight-year-old me would've freaked out because he looked so much like one of the Banksia Men from *Snugglepot and Cuddlepie*. It wouldn't have surprised me to learn that his beard was a completely separate organism engaged in a symbiotic relationship with its host.

'Hi Mr P,' I say.

'Got a good one today,' he says. 'Going to dip our heads in the creek, see what's biting.'

'Good thing I brought my shower cap, then.'

'No worries at all, Clancy. No worries at all.' Mr P has a habit of responding to a sentence that you haven't actually said. He gives me this weird look, like he's trying to read something on my forehead. 'Head up to the tank, hey,' he says. 'Be up in a sec.'

I walk out of the office, rubbing my brow. There's probably Vegemite up there. I have a talent for that. Mr P's left the gate unlatched so I push it open, stepping up onto its base so it swings me out with it. There's all these awesome warning signs stuck to the gate about hazardous chemicals and fruit flies and fire ants. I jump over the cattle grid and go over to the shed where you have to clean the soles of your shoes in a tray of detergent.

I can see the others up at the Tank, a big green reservoir the size of a small house that supplies all the water to the station. Everyone's here already. Back when the club started, back when Angus was in it, every kid wanted to be part of it.

I joined, of course, just as it was becoming uncool, just as everyone suddenly realised they could hang out at the skate ramp or at the Bellie Park grandstand and waste their lives. Now—as much as I never admit it out loud— Nature Club is the sole refuge of loners, nerds and general misfits.

There are seven of us who come regularly, but we're such an awkward group, I've never really considered us 'friends'. Nathan and Andrea I know because they're in my grade in school and Glenn is a few grades above. There's a brother and sister, Tom and Olive, who are home-schooled and one younger kid who never talks and who in my head I call DD, because he always wears denim overalls over a denim shirt. Mainly, we don't talk unless Mr P's there.

I wave to them as I walk over, keeping my head down, like *hello everybody at once so I don't have to say hello individually.* No one says anything, except Nancy.

'Hi Clancy!' she says.

Nancy is new. It's only the second time she's come to Nature Club. She's just moved here and she's starting school next term, in my grade. She's bright and loud and friendly and I have no idea what she's doing with us.

'Hi Nancy.'

'Hi Clancy!' she says. 'It's pretty funny, hey. Nancy, Clancy.' A joke already very tired. She laughs a bubbly laugh and I hate her. I don't need anyone bubbly this morning. I need good old-fashioned silence and social awkwardness. Nature Club usually delivers this in spades.

'You look like you haven't had your coffee yet,' Nancy says, one hand on her hip. It's the same pose I've seen girls at school do. Taken from some sitcom where eye-rolling and freezing your body at hieroglyphic angles is considered the height of wit.

'Something like that,' I say.

'I know *I* need my caffeine!'

I give her a look, like, *just because our names rhyme doesn't mean you shouldn't piss right off.* She's been trying to buddy up to me ever since she arrived.

'How's your week been, anyway?' she says.

'Fine.'

Finally, thankfully, DD sniffs up a massive booger and normality returns.

Glenn says, 'I—I wonder what Professor Parry has in store for us this morning?' Glenn has air moss hair and wiggles his fingers every time he speaks. 'Perhaps the wonders of the turbidity wheel.' Glenn is the oldest of us and has perfected the sort of deep, affected sardonic tone reserved for the serious *Star Trek* fan and the relentlessly teased.

Mercifully, Mr P then clomps up behind us, rubbing his hands together. 'Right then,' he says. 'Let's get to work.' He hands out these plastic discs with long lengths of string attached. Glenn makes a humming noise because apparently, yes, these are turbidity wheels.

'You all got your notebooks?' says Mr P.

Everyone nods except for me. Crap. A notebook, Mr P often tells us, is a scientist's most important tool. Nancy, who's standing next to me, says, 'You can have some of mine,' and rips out a bunch of pages from her expensive-looking journal.

'Thanks,' I say, my cheeks going red as she hands them to me.

George Parry runs us through the morning's experiment and as he does I realise I haven't even brought a hat or sunscreen or any of the things I always remember to pack the night before. For some reason this really unsettles me, and as Mr P's talking I'm not listening because I'm trying not to cry. I pinch myself on the leg, like *harden up, you idiot*, but it just makes it worse. I don't want to cry. I don't want to be the person who stands out. I don't want to rely on someone else. I think about last night. Mum's face. The desperation in her voice. What happened to Dad? Why was—

'All clear, then?' George Parry claps his hands and I nod automatically.

I try to breathe. I want to be back home, in my room, face down on my bed.

'All good, Clancy?' Mr P. says. 'Know what we're doing?'

Everyone's staring at me like I'm an alien. I must look terrible.

I feel Nancy grab my hand. She says, 'We'll do ours together. We'll have to share a pen.'

'Thanks,' I say, and am astonished when I realise I actually mean it.

*The creek's a* five-minute walk away, behind the last building of the station. Mr P holds down the loose wire of the fence so we can step over it and follow the unofficial track down into the valley. None of us says anything about how different the back entrance to the station is from the front. No warning signs on the fence. No disinfectant.

On the way to the creek I drop behind the others, but Nancy stays with me.

'You okay?' she says.

'Yeah.' I'm still fighting the overwhelming urge to cry. 'I'm just…I'm just tired.'

'Fair enough. Nothing that can't be cured by *the wonders of the turbidity wheel*, though.' She wiggles her fingers like Glenn.

Despite myself, I smile. 'Thanks for the lend of the paper,' I say, holding out the torn pages.

'That's okay.' Nancy spins her wheel in front of her, its black and white segments whirring together into grey.

We make our way down the slope together in silence until she says, 'I don't want to, um—if you want to walk by yourself, that's cool.'

'No, it's okay.'

'I just—it's that thing where you've lived somewhere your whole life and then you have to start again.' She keeps spinning the wheel until the string gets tangled up. 'I've never had to, you know, *make friends*. I just sort of…collected them back in Brisbane. When you grow up together or you have neighbours or whatever.' She squints up at the sky. 'Sorry, I'm talking about nothing. I tend to do that.'

'It's fine,' I say. 'Don't worry about it. I can imagine…' Could I imagine? At least in Barwen, I guess, I know where everything is and how everything sort of works. I think about all the stuff you'd have to learn again if you moved. Still, why anyone would move *to* Barwen is beyond me.

'Your mum came for work, right?' I say.

'Yeah. The boarding school. Vice Principal.'

'Ugh, all those boys cooped up together.'

'I know.'

'What did she do in Brisbane?'

'She was teaching, but, um, she needed a change.'

'So she came here?' I open my eyes wide, like *really?*

'Well…I mean, is Barwen that bad?'

I pause for a moment. 'It's worse.'

'Oh.' Nancy's voice falters for a moment. She slows down.

41

I look back at her and she seems momentarily deflated. 'It's not *all* bad, though,' I say, feeling sorry for her. 'I know who does the best hot chips. I've done a fairly comprehensive survey.' This elicits a small smile. I like Nancy a lot more now I can see her positivity isn't permanent. 'Also, at the video shop, which we somehow still have, there's this loophole where you can basically get a free overnight if you do it right.'

'Wow,' she says. 'Just like in Paris.'

I snort. 'Exactly like Paris. And you've got to know which public toilets you should *never* visit, which is pretty much all of them.'

Nancy lets out a big laugh and I'm about to keep going with the joke but I catch myself. She's got these huge eyes which I've just noticed. I think about the stupid clothes I'm wearing and how I've had no sleep and how I must look like an escapee from a high-security scarecrow prison. Was Nancy laughing *with* me, or *at* me? Will she get on the phone tonight and laugh about me to her Brisbane friends?

She gives me a weird look because my face must be scrunching up like it does when I let my train of thought run me over.

'You okay?' she says. 'You disappeared for a second there.'

'Sorry, I was just thinking about something.' Full Disney princess voice. Bloody hell.

Nancy smiles again. 'Nothing too serious, I hope.'

'Just family shi— family stuff.' I've said the words before I realise they're out of my mouth. Why would I tell her this?

She throws the disc over her shoulder. 'Family stuff's the worst. Take it from me.'

By this time we've reached the creek and George Parry's there with everyone else. A full nerd encampment. In my head, it's always *the nerds*, as if I'm not part of it, as if I'm not comfortable around them because they remind me so much of myself. Nancy will see this soon. She'll realise she's accidentally booked a one-way trip to the Geek Islands, and she'll want to fly straight home. I belong with people who make me feel slightly good about myself because they exist only as a collection of ridiculous details—science puns and double-denim and bowl cuts— and I can pretend I'm the cool kid.

I go over and stand next to Glenn, who tips his cap back, points to a tree and says, 'Number one. The larch,' which I know is from Monty Python but today I ignore it. Nancy comes over and joins us, and George Parry starts talking about the day's experiment but I can't stop my brain now. My thoughts are tumbling around like socks in a washing machine. A little heart jump at the idea that Nancy would become *a friend*, soon cancelled out by what I know is reality, that when school starts up she'll immediately be adopted by the popular kids. Anyone from a town bigger than Barwen is pure gold to them, anything that suggests sophistication and glamour and all that Sex and the City bullshit they'll never have but eternally pretend they will.

'That all make sense?' says George Parry.

Everyone nods, and Tom and Olive are already writing in their matching notebooks. I pretend to follow along, but I'm already hating today. Hating Nature Club, the one place in the world I thought was a purely hate-free zone.

*I spend the* rest of the day in my room, which isn't unusual in itself, but I can tell Dad's still home because I hear the shower going some time late in the afternoon. I assume he's on a late shift, but I don't hear his boots on the stairs or the sound of the car starting up. I hear Angus shouting at Titch downstairs, Titch screaming back, Mum trying to calm them down. It's super weird for all of us to be home at once, especially in the holidays. I try to block out my family—and my own swirling thoughts—by lying on the bed, under the doona, with music turned up loud on my headphones and holding a fantastically bad biography on Dolly Parton I got from the library way too close to my face so I can read it which is fine because there is no way I'm getting glasses on top of everything else. I'm listening to a playlist I've made called *Good/Hopeful Heartbreak*.

Some time around five pm, Angus bursts into my room.

'Get out,' I say automatically. We have an agreement,

my brother and I. Neither of us goes into the other's room, *ever*, and this way both of us avoid the inevitable destruction of our favourite possessions.

'We gotta be downstairs.'

I pretend not to hear him. 'I said *get out*.'

'Seriously. You gotta be downstairs now.'

'Fine where I am, thanks.'

Angus doesn't throw anything at me or punch my leg, which is usually his next move. He just goes, 'Clancy. Seriously.'

This is when I know something's actually up. I take off my headphones. 'What's going on?'

'You just...you just gotta come downstairs.'

He walks out of my room and I throw on a jumper and slippers. Even before I get downstairs and walk into the lounge room, I know this has something to do with last night. I suppose I've been waiting for it.

Angus is on the big sofa and Mum's on one of the lounge chairs. Dad's in his recliner, slumped down. He's got bruises and cuts all down his legs. He looks up when I come into the room and...he's been crying. His eyes are all red and his hair's still wet from the shower. He doesn't say anything, just stares at a point somewhere over my shoulder. My heart starts going a million miles a minute. It's a scene so familiar—Dad, after work, crashed on the couch, wearing footy shorts and the threadbare singlet his old cricket team printed up for their end-of-season trip— but everything about it is wrong.

Angus says, 'She's here, okay? So what's going on?'

'Give me a second, mate,' says Dad, the first words I've heard him say for days.

'Okay,' says Angus. 'I'm just—I don't know—worried.' It's weird to hear him talking quietly.

'Darl?' Mum looks over to Dad, who doesn't meet her eyes. I can see the baby-white of his scalp between the wet spikes of his hair.

'Can you sit down, Clancy?'

'Where's Titch?'

'He's in his room. He…can you just sit down, please. Now.' She puts on her forceful teacher's voice. I sit down next to Angus on the sofa. 'Your dad's been involved in an accident,' Mum says. 'Yesterday. On the highway.'

'Jesus,' is all I can say.

'I'm fine,' says Dad in a monotone. His eyes are still fixed on the back of the room.

'The car okay?' says Angus, and I punch him in the arm. 'I mean, shit. As long as *you're* okay.' He tries to catch Dad's eye. 'That dickhead Buggs was shouting something about you. When we were driving back last night.'

'Angus!' Mum glares at my brother.

'Shit,' says Dad. 'Shit, shit, shit.' He puts his head in his hands.

Mum gets up and goes over to him. 'It's okay, darl.' She rubs his back, going around in circles, and it's the only sound we can hear.

'Anyone else hurt?' says Angus.

47

'I don't want to talk about it,' Dad says. 'Don't know why we're all here like it's a bloody courtroom.'

'Bob, *please*.' Mum stares at him like she can make him look up, but he doesn't. 'I want them to hear it from you, rather than from someone else who doesn't know what they're talking about.'

My pulse hammers my temples.

'It's nothing,' Dad says. 'It's fine.' But then he lifts his head. He looks so faded. 'Actually, it's not fine. It really isn't.' His eyes suddenly look so dry that I close mine, rubbing them. He says, 'I was in...involved in an accident. I'm fine. But two people died. Two...young people.' He scratches at his singlet and a moment later a patch of red appears, just below where his old nickname, *Tucka,* is printed. 'I was working. Out on the highway. Traffic control. These two kids. Not kids, but...your age, teenagers. Driving.'

Now I'm just staring at him like, *holy shit.*

Dad rubs his eyes and his uneven breath tells me he's about to cry. 'They went past me. There was a grader. They didn't...' He starts to sniff violently. He notices the stain on his singlet. 'Fucker won't stop bleeding.'

I remember the red smear I noticed on Dad's work shirt. I steal a glance at Angus, who looks just as confused as me.

'I was on duty,' says Dad. 'That time of night, there's only one car every half hour. We'd closed a lane. They just shot through. The grader's this huge bloody truck and

48

of course you can't hear anything when you're driving it. These kids in the car, they clip it and go off the embankment. You can't...' He stands up. 'I need a drink.'

Mum says, 'I can put some dinner on.'

'Not hungry,' Dad says. 'I'm going out back.' He stands up, looking unsteady on his feet. His bowed, hairy legs.

'Darl, can you just stay for—'

'Nah, I gotta go.' He staggers out of the room and we hear the back door bang its familiar triple-rattle.

It feels like it isn't real, like it's a dream or I've fainted or something. My brain can't catch up.

'What the hell?' goes Angus. 'What happened? Why's he bleeding?'

Mum smooths down her pants. 'The main thing is he's fine.'

'So these kids in the car,' says Angus. 'They didn't *run into* Dad. He let them through? They went straight into this grader?'

'It's very sad, yes.' Mum keeps nodding her head.

'So why's he look like he's been in a car crash? His legs all cut up and shit?' Angus's voice is back to usual, the tone that means he thinks he knows better than everyone else.

'He tried to help them, Angus. The car went off the road. He tried to get them out of the car.'

We hear the grumble of the shed's rollerdoor from the backyard. The whack as it slams back down.

'Which way was it facing?' I say.

Mum's mouth wavers. 'Which way was *what* facing?'

'His sign.'

Mum sighs, her lips making a *pah* sound before releasing the air. Her sound. She doesn't answer.

'Was he telling the cars to stop or go?' I've got tears stinging my eyes.

'I don't know, sweetie.'

'Did he tell you which way?'

She shakes her head.

'Jesus,' says Angus. 'Jesus.'

*I have dreams* full of flying knives and wake up early all knotted into my bedding and the air smells like too-ripe fruit. I untangle myself from my sheets. There's something deeper to the smell, an unfamiliar chemical edge. I've left my window open a crack and I realise the smell's coming through it. I pull back the curtains and it's only just light, but already there's something not quite right with the front yard.

One of the sleepers that line the sides of the driveway is off-kilter and then I see the glint of something red right below the window and I shank a breath because it's my bike, its frame mangled up, the front wheel bent at a mad angle. It's been run over, clearly. More than once.

I throw on a jumper and run downstairs and when I open the door I realise quickly the chemical smell is fresh paint. All along our front wall, partially covering one window, someone's sprayed *MURDRER*.

My heart falters and I want to be sick. I bend down

until the nausea passes and go down the front steps and over to my broken bike. It's covered with dew and there's big scratches in the paint. *Lighting Lady* is finally dead. Even though so many of my waking hours have been spent devising ways to destroy her, the reality isn't quite as satisfying as I'd hoped.

Buggs, or his dipshit crew. My bike must've fallen off right in front of them when we went past the Cri the other night. I turn around and see someone's sprayed a skull and crossbones next to *MURDRER*. I get a weird thrill when my brain goes, *maybe Sasha did it.* She wouldn't have, though. She would've stayed in the car while Buggs and them tagged the house and dragged my bike up the yard. She would've just stared at her reflection in the adjusted rearview mirror. The idea that she's been so close to me, though, is exciting and horrible at the same time.

I step back and put my bare foot on the slimy cling-film wrapped around our morning paper. I sit on the front step and unwrap it, carefully peeling back the sticky layers of plastic. The thin tabloid of the *Barwen Chronicle* unfurls and there, on the front page, are two giant words: *Highway Tragedy*. The accident would've happened after yesterday's paper went to print, but they've wasted no time making up for it. There's never any real news in the *Chronicle*, so when there is they go all out.

There are two pictures below the headline and it shocks me to recognise the unmistakable colouring of our school photos, that awful mottled grey background. We only had them taken a few weeks ago, before we broke up for summer. The driver was in year twelve and I only knew him by his face. *Charles Jencke*. Blond, good-looking. He was on the footy and swimming teams and he had an acne streak that ran down from his fringe to the top of his cheekbone.

I don't need to read the caption under the other photo. Everyone knew who she was. Everyone knew Cassandra Lamaire. Top of the class, top of the school. She was always in the paper. The front page for science camps and academic medals. The back page for athletics carnivals and trips to state championships for middle-distance running. Always *Olympic hopeful Cassandra Lamaire*. Barwen royalty in the way Buggs and his family could never be.

'Shit,' I say under my breath. I skim the article for Dad's name but it isn't there. There's a quote from the mayor saying how two lives have been 'cut short too soon'. A few lines from the police about road safety, about an 'ongoing investigation'. I flick through the rest of the paper, but can't see any mention of Dad. Thank God. Buggs knew, though. His uncle was a cop, but even if he wasn't, gossip works so fast in Barwen that Buggs would've found out soon enough. It'll be all over town by the middle of the day.

'You shouldn't keep the door open.'

I swing around and Titch is there in his awful Spongebob pyjamas that Mum can never convince him to throw out. 'Get inside,' I say.

'*You* get inside.'

'Why don't we have some breakfast?' I get up fast to block his view but he peers past me.

'Why's your bike all bashed up? Dad'll be steaming.' He grins.

'Doesn't matter. Let's go inside.' I put my hands on his shoulders but he doesn't move. His body is solid pudge, honed to deadweight perfection by a life spent in pursuit of sugar.

'Why's it smell weird?'

'It doesn't smell weird. Get inside.'

He tries to step out and I block him again.

'What's out there?'

'Nothing.' We're in an official grapple now, and I know my stick-figure frame is no match for him so I pinch his arm and when he lets go of me I knock him over.

'OWWW!' Titch makes it sound like I've chopped off one of his fingers. 'That *really* hurt!'

I slam the door behind me. 'It's too early,' I say. 'We don't need to be up yet.'

'You hurt me! I'm telling Mum.'

Jesus Christ. 'Let's get some breakfast, hey?'

'MUM!' Titch shouts, still lying on the floor, 'CLANCY PUNCHED ME AND PUSHED ME OVER AND IT REALLY HURT!'

'You're such a little baby. I didn't even punch you.' I realise then I've left the paper outside.

Mum appears at the top of the stairs with almost

superhuman speed. Her hair's a bird's nest of dirty blonde. 'Do you know what time it is?' she says.

'CLANCY PUNCHED ME.'

'Mum, I need to talk to you.'

'SHE PUNCHED ME!'

'I don't care,' says Mum. 'Your father is trying to sleep after an awful few days and you two are making noise like animals.' She grabs at her head. 'Just keep quiet.'

'Mum, I need to talk to you. It's about…what happened.' My brain fizzes.

'Darling, I can't right now. I just need another hour's sleep, and then we can deal with it.'

'CAN I WATCH CARTOONS?'

I close my eyes. Why is this crap always on *me*? 'I was *trying* to keep Titch inside,' I say, 'because someone's spray-painted our front wall.'

'Cool!'

'Shut up, Titch.'

Mum's hand falls to her side. 'What?'

'And my bike. Someone's run over it. It's busted it up and they left it in the front yard.'

'I see.' Mum gathers up her dressing gown, changes her voice into a teacher's. 'Titch, you can watch cartoons but keep the volume down.'

'Sweet!' Titch springs up, his debilitating injuries magically vanishing.

Mum comes down the stairs.

'What does the graffiti say?' Her face is scrunched up

like she's thought of something disgusting.

'It's not spelled very well,' I say.

She pushes past me and goes out onto the verandah. Her face goes white. 'Oh no,' she says. 'Oh no. Do *not* tell your father.' Her finger's pointing at me like I've already told him.

'The paper's there too. His name isn't in it.' I pick it up from the front step and hand it to her.

She scans the front page, the disgusted look never once leaving her face. 'We've got to clean this up,' she says. 'We've got to get rid of this before your dad gets up.'

'What about my bike? How am I going to get to work?'

'Put it under the house or something.' Mum looks at the graffiti again. 'Bloody monsters.'

Mum has to drop me into town for work and the whole way she keeps asking me if I'm sure I want to go. We spent nearly an hour trying to clean off the graffiti and we both still smell of metho.

'I'm fine,' I keep telling her. 'It's fine.'

'But you don't have to, sweetie. Not with everything that's going on.'

'There's no one else who can work, though.' This isn't entirely true. Eloise could probably easily have worked today. There was no way I was staying home, though. The atmosphere was toxic and without my bike, work was my only way out.

Mum hits me with a few greeting-card racks' worth of motivational quotes before we finally arrive. She parks a few blocks away from the shopping centre entrance.

'Now you stay strong today, Clancy. Don't forget, you're a wonderful person.'

'Right. Yep.' I make my escape, reaching into the back

seat for my backpack so I don't have to make the moment last any longer.

'Remember your soul is only—'

I slam the door. I feel bad about this, but only slightly. One of the best things we learned in physics is how *nature abhors a vacuum*. Mum, in one of her manic moods, is pretty much the same. She keeps talking to fill up any empty space.

I walk through the sliding doors and straight away realise the shopping centre's air-conditioning has broken down again. Instead of the usual wave of coolness there's stifling warm air. Bloody great. The air-con breaks down at least once a month, and it means people are going to be in shitty moods which means I'll sell even less than usual which means six hours of complete and utter boredom.

I raise an eyebrow at Knife Guy, but he looks like today has already defeated him. Pewter-handled letter-openers and the trapped heat of a couple of hundred people, not a great combination. I go up the escalators and everyone I see looks tired and worn out. I slump up to the Beauty Station and get a shock when I see Eloise standing behind the counter.

'Did I get the roster wrong?'

'No darling,' she says. 'I just had some things to do.'

'Oh okay.' I stash my backpack away. Now I don't even have the station set-up—which I can usually stretch out to a good hour—to delay the boredom. If I was by myself I could pass the time in my own way. With Eloise hovering over me, it means thousands of menial tasks.

'I am taking stock, darling,' she says. 'Inventory.' She's got on this tiny black jacket over her blouse that doesn't really seem to serve any purpose other than to restrict the movement of her arms.

'Didn't you do inventory last week?'

'But you know, darling, it is a job that is never finished. Every day you sell more, our stock changes, and *wallah*!' She snaps her fingers.

'I suppose. But I can finish set-up. You could get a coffee, or...'

'No no no. There is always so much to be done!' She touches me on the side of the face, brushing my hair lightly. I shudder, but not because it's unpleasant. Her perfume is musky and perfect.

I start to put out the sample boxes and make up the float. One of the starburst-shaped price signs has fallen apart so I start to make up a new one. All the time, Eloise ticks her pen against her clipboard behind me, doing sums in her head.

'Darling,' she says eventually. 'Tell me. How are you this morning?'

I turn around. 'Good thanks. How are you?'

'I am fine, you know, above my aches and pains.' Eloise rubs her hip: part of a catalogue of mysterious European ailments she often alludes to. She says, 'I do not wish to pry, darling, but I have heard about your father. A terrible accident.'

My skin tightens. It makes sense now. Why she's come in early. 'Well, yeah,' I say. 'It's...not good.'

She puts a hand on my arm. 'I am sure it will be all right, Clancy. You tell him I'm thinking of him, and if there is anything I can do to help...' She trails off, in the way you sort of have to when you're offering condolences.

I'm actually struggling then to think of when her and Dad would've met. I want to ask how she knows about Dad's involvement in the accident, but it's not too hard to work out. Eloise and the local florist—a tiny loud lady called Gaby who wears gaping linen shirts—have a regular wine date each afternoon at the Cri, sitting in the corner, shrieking with laughter. Gaby is the central cog in Barwen's gossip machine.

'Thanks,' I say. 'I'm sure everything'll be fine.' I start to think—worryingly—that maybe Mum was right. Maybe I should've stayed home.

We spend the first few hours with no customers and I alphabetise the already perfectly ordered sample cards and wipe down the Hollywood mirror—trying more than ever to avoid my reflection, my crumpled car-door hair and mouth-full-of-toothpaste face—and all the while Eloise doesn't seem to do any inventory checks but instead stares off into the depths of the shopping centre, tapping the pen intermittently on the clipboard. She clucks her tongue at people as they walk past and soon I realise some of them are regular customers.

I start to observe a worrying pattern, which is

confirmed just before midday when our first customer of the day finally approaches us. It's a woman called Raylene McCarthy, who has facial eczema and swears by an expensive cream Eloise recommended to her. She comes up to the counter pushing a shopping trolley containing her rat-tailed twins Bronson and Braden. They're both little turds who're in the same grade as Titch, but who make my brother look like a model citizen. Back when I was into skateboarding—by which I mean dressing like a skater—I hung out with their older brother Troy, who was pretty cool. But these kids...jeez.

'Raylene,' says Eloise, upping her accent. 'How are you, my darlink? How are my little *bambinos*? Growing so fast!' She waves to the twins, who just stare back, breathing through their mouths. They try to rock the trolley over.

'Stop it you two!' Raylene waves a lazy open palm behind her, catching Braden on his ear.

'What can I do for you today?' Eloise says to Raylene. 'Your skin is looking wonderful but I have some new serum from France that could light you up!'

Raylene squints up one eye, the other trained squarely on me. 'Eloise,' she says. 'I would just like to register my extreme disappointment.' Eloise begins to respond but Raylene holds up a starfish hand. 'I think in light of *recent events*, it's in poor taste to continue to employ *certain people*.'

'*Excuse moi?*' Eloise puts down her clipboard.

'No offence to you, Eloise,' says Raylene, 'but I will not be shopping here while you continue to employ *certain people.*' She swivels both her blackcurrant eyes to Eloise and half-grins like she's super proud of her tact. 'I'm sure you understand.'

'Is that so?' Eloise's voice changes. It's slower and suddenly deeper.

'Yes, that is so. There are certain elements in this town that need to be discouraged, and I'm not the only one who feels this way. We shall not be supporting businesses who choose to side with certain elements.'

I try my best to stay calm, to not look at anyone, but my heart is nearly thumping through my chest. Bronson has his hands down his pants, rummaging around his Jim Beam shorts with the manic concentration of a hopeful prospector. I hope he breaks it off.

'Let me make one thing clear to you,' says Eloise, stabbing the air with her pen, 'I do not, nor have I ever, supported *any* level of discrimination or small-mindedness. I respect of course your right to shop where you want, but I disagree one hundred per cent with your reasons for doing so. You can tell anybody you like that I will not be changing any staff here. I will continue, with my current sales force, to sell beauty products of the highest quality to anyone who wishes to buy them.'

Raylene doesn't say anything for a moment, then scratches her cheek with a quick movement. Her skin flakes off like fancy salt. She didn't expect Eloise to react like this. She clearly thought her tabloid consumer-power bluff would not be called. 'It's all overpriced anyway,' she says, huffing out her words. 'You're welcome to her.' She flicks her hand at me. 'Underhills have always been trouble. Tucka's been a bad egg since forever. A criminal element we don't need.'

Right, I think, that's bloody it. I go to move out through the swinging door at the side of the counter but Eloise grabs my arm with a surprisingly strong grip. I snap my head around but she just signals to me with a lowered palm, like, *it's not worth it.*

Raylene huffs and turns away. She tries to swing the trolley around back the way she's come but the twins use their instinctive grasp of resistance physics to push all their weight the other way, rendering the trolley impossible to move. I snort a laugh but Raylene—clearly used to the behaviour of her shithead sons—pushes the front of the trolley instead and wheels it briskly backwards towards the supermarket.

'Thanks,' I say to Eloise. 'You didn't have to, you know...'

'The ignorance of this town sometimes!' Eloise slaps her forehead. 'I am sorry you had to hear that.'

'It's fine.' I smooth down my shirt like I'm dusting myself off. 'She's probably right, though. Maybe I shouldn't be the, um, face of the business for a little while.'

'Nonsense! There is nothing wrong with you working here.'

'But you heard her. Everyone's going to think the same thing. I mean, no one's come to the counter all morning.'

'It will be fine, darling. People will forget about this whole episode in no time.'

'Maybe. But I don't want to hurt your business.'

Eloise nods. 'It's your choice darling. But please know that I will always want you here.'

My heart breaks. She's one of the good ones. Which is why I say, 'I just need to probably be with Mum and Dad. For a little bit.' Which is sort of true. Maybe.

*It's only as* I'm walking back through the shopping centre that I remember I have no bike and therefore no way of getting home. I'm convinced everyone I walk past is looking at me, judging me and my family. There's no way *everyone* can already know, is there? Surely not everyone can think my dad is guilty without even knowing the whole story? For crying out loud, *I* don't even know the whole story.

I get a strawberry Big M from a vending machine, even though they're cheaper in the supermarket, and go outside to sit on one of the benches near the bakery. It's so much cooler in the open air. My makeup feels separated from my face by a layer of sweat. I find a napkin in my backpack and wipe as much off as I can. I pull out my iPod—a hand-me-down from Angus with a grey screen so scratched up you can hardly see what song's playing—and navigate to a playlist called *Shitty Day 14*. My *Shitty Day* playlists, of which there are nearly thirty, are not—as you might think—filled with songs designed to make me feel better, but rather songs that celebrate sadness and pity. The first one I titled *Now That's What I Call Suicidal!* but I thought it was a little over the top.

I lean back on the bench and close my eyes, letting the music wash over me. A heavy weight lands beside me and I jolt alert to see a big blue uniform sitting beside me and inside it Security Officer Reeve Lewis. He points to my Big M. 'A good drop, that.'

I nod. 'Aged in a vending machine for six months. Really develops the complexity of flavour.'

Reeve takes off his cap and puts it in his lap. 'Working today?'

'Sort of. Well, no. I was. I'm about to go home.'

'You all right?'

'Yeah. Just this...thing. The accident.' I still don't know how to refer to it.

'Oh yeah. Right. How's your dad?'

'He's okay.'

'It's crazy,' says Reeve. 'I used to play footy with CJ. He was a good guy.'

'CJ?'

'Charlie Jencke. You probably didn't know him. He was a year below me. Good winger.'

Reeve left school in year ten, which often makes people assume he's stupid, or lazy or something. He isn't either as far as I can tell. He's a nice guy, and funny. One of the few people I'd consider a friend, even though he's two years older than me. 'Everyone thinks Dad had something to do with it,' I say. 'Cause he was out on the road.'

Reeve shrugs. 'Who knows what's what? It's just sad. And Cassie, Cassandra Whatsername. She was like, a freak. With her sport and school stuff and whatever.'

'It is sad,' I say. 'But some people...well, so, I was supposed to be working today but Raylene McCarthy— you know, with the twins? She comes up and says no one wants to shop at the Beauty Station because of me.'

'Really? That's insane.'

'I know. Eloise was there so she calmed it down. I would've clocked her flaky face otherwise. I feel bad for Eloise. I don't want her to lose business.'

Reeve shakes his head. 'Those McCarthy twins. I had to pull one out of one of the public toilets once. He just climbed in and got his foot stuck.'

'Shoulda left him there.'

'Too right.' Reeve looks at his watch. 'You heading off now?'

'Yeah.' I don't want to tell Reeve about my bike, or the graffiti. Not that I don't trust him, but I know Mum'd be mortified if the spray-paint thing got around town. 'Might be off work for a couple of days.'

'Oh, right.' There seems to be genuine disappointment in Reeve's voice. 'Well if there's anything I can do...'

'Thanks, man. I'll let you know.'

'Oh, hey, before you go.' Reeve reaches into his jacket. 'Quiet day at the print shop. Tran let me make these.'

He hands me a small card. It says *Clancy Underhill: Vice-Deputy Beauty Consultant* and is surrounded by a horrible border of stock-image illustrated clowns.

Reeve says, 'Only the flimsiest paper, of course. Only the least legible font.'

I laugh. 'Finally I can begin my climb up the corporate ladder.'

'Check it out, though.' He hands me another one. The same font, but this time *Reeve Lewis: Senior Executive Retail Law Enforcement Officer, Esq.* He's got jet fighters flanking his name, and below it, his mobile number. 'Pretty sweet, right?'

'Have you actually been handing these out?'

'Not yours. That's a limited edition. But I've given out a few of mine. Gotta grow my brand awareness.'

'You idiot.'

I'm about to get up when I notice Buggs's Monaro driving towards us. My stomach twists. The car slows down, and I can't see if Sasha is in there because the windows are up and they're tinted polaroid blue. There's an empty car space up ahead and I pray that the car doesn't stop. It looks like it's gone past, but at the last minute it swings in. The engine growls before it shuts off. I stuff the business cards into my pants pocket. 'Can you stay here for one sec?' I say to Reeve.

'Sure,' he says. 'What's up?'

I don't answer. Instead I watch Buggs stoop out from the driver's seat, taking off his cap, smoothing back his hair. He comes towards us, leaning backwards as he walks like he's moving against a headwind. 'Nice day for it,' he says, winking at me. 'Got up early, myself. Couldn't wait to greet the day.' His pushed-down nose makes him look like a scared whippet.

'Hi *Barnaby*,' I say.

Buggs picks something from between his teeth. Rubs the back of the hand over his harelip scar. '*Clancy*,' he says slowly, drawing out the A. 'Strange name for a chick. Clancy Underhill. Not a great name.'

'Better than Barney Pfister, anyway,' I say quietly.

'That's the thing about names,' says Buggs. 'They gotta lot of meaning to them. Like *Underhill*. In this town, that name means *shit*.'

Reeve crosses his arms. 'You got better things to do, Buggs?'

'Not really, retard. You?'

Reeve just sits there, staring at Buggs.

Buggs laughs. 'Yeah, should get going. Gotta lot of work on. Heading down to Bellie Park, smoke some cones.' He covers his mouth in mock-shock. 'Ah no, you gonna arrest me for that?' He holds out his wrists. 'Slap 'em on me.'

'Piss off,' says Reeve.

'Yeah, whatever. I'm not the one going to jail anyway. Hear the cops are on the trail of a murderer. Killed that kid and his missus night before last.' Buggs whistles. 'Double murder. That's heavy.'

I can't say anything. Suddenly I see Dad in jail. Not in a cell, but out in the exercise yard. Orange jumpsuit and a scared look in his eyes. I can't get the image out of my head. My hands start shaking so I turn them into fists to make them stop.

Reeve stands up, drawing up his full bulk. He says, 'Piss. Off.' It sound like he means it.

Buggs laughs. 'Scary stuff.' He raises his hands like he's surrendering. 'I'm gone. I'm gone. See ya in the papers.' He winks at me once more with his weird dog face. He gets back into his car, starts it up and reverses out of the spot with another growl of the engine.

Reeve sits back down next to me. 'You okay?' he says.

'Yeah. He's a douchebag.'

'Massive. Don't listen to him, anyway. He's just winding you up.'

'Yeah. Thanks for sticking around.'

'Any time, Clance. You know that.' He checks his watch again. 'Sure you're okay?'

'Yeah. He's all talk.'

'Okay. I gotta go. Time waits for no tan. A wise girl taught me that.'

'You should listen to her,' I say. 'Definitely.'

*I'm still shaking* as I walk up to the payphone outside the Cri. I know Buggs is just being a dick as usual, but I can't get the image of Dad in prison out of my head. The worst I'd thought up until now was that he might lose his job and we'd have to live off Mum's salary again like we did when Dad's council compo ran out last time. Mum had to keep going further and further out of town to get supply work, getting home after Titch had gone to bed. The first time I realised how close to being povo we really were. The first time I'd actually worried about it. For some reason, up until now the worst-case scenario hasn't yet entered my head: that Dad is actually guilty, that because he didn't do his job...because of him two kids are dead.

The Cri is officially closed at this time of the morning, but already the shutters are open and there are two grey-faced regulars death-gripping schooners.

The payphone is one of the last ones left in town, with

a furry Yellow Pages hanging off the wall on a chain. I go to pick up the handset and it's then I realise I've spent the last of my money on the Big M and I stand there for a few moments listening to the dial tone as if it's going to tell me how to fix this. Mum won't be coming to pick me up for another four hours. Angus and I aren't allowed to get mobiles unless we pay for them ourselves, which makes times like this even worse. Angus won't get one because of some crackpot fear of radiation and government tracking, and all the money I earn goes towards saving for a car.

I lean forward and rest my head on the top of the payphone. It's probably covered with germs but at this stage I don't really care. I'll have to wait or walk home or ask someone for money and all I want is to be face down on my doona. Why isn't anything easy? I feel the tears coming on and they're bastards because the more I try to stop them the quicker they arrive.

'Clancy?'

A familiar voice, and possibly the last person I want to speak to at this particular moment.

'Clancy, are you okay?'

I keep my forehead pressed to the top of the phone, the dial tone transformed to a repeated bleep, urging me to make a decision.

'Clancy?' A hand on my shoulder.

I lift my head up and there's Nancy. Behind her is someone I can only assume is her mum. They're both wearing dresses, proper dresses with properly nice modern patterns, the type you can't and never will be able to buy in Barwen.

'Hello,' I say. 'How are you both this morning?' For some reason, I've gone super formal, as if because they're both dressed nicely they'll want to speak like a Jane Austen character.

'We're good,' says Nancy. 'I just saw you in the phone booth here, and wanted to check...'

Wanted to check why I was leaning my head against something that has probably been vomited on twice in the last twelve hours? Bloody good question. I sniff and wipe my eyes with the edges of my thumbs, in the time-honoured tradition of people who have been caught crying and are trying to pretend they haven't been.

'I was just trying to call Mum for a lift and then realised I didn't have any money.' I shrug, like *you know how it is*, even though I'm one hundred per cent sure Nancy doesn't know how this is. She has probably never used a payphone.

'Oh, well do you need a lift somewhere?' Nancy has on sunglasses that reflect my face back at me.

'Absolutely,' says Nancy's mum. 'It's Clancy, isn't it. I'm Carla, Nancy's mum.'

'Yes,' I say. 'I mean, yes, that's my name. Not yes that's *your* name...' My brain's like *just stop talking*. 'It's nice to meet you.'

'We're just on our way home ourselves,' Carla says.

'It's fine,' I say. 'Thanks, though.'

'Nonsense,' says Carla. 'It's no trouble.'

I don't even know where Nancy lives, but it's probably straight out of an architectural magazine. Heated floors, cooled walls, whatever it is rich people have to make their lives easier. There is no way they're going to see *my* house. 'I'll probably just walk,' I say, as another fat tear sneaks up on me. I wipe it away and my hand comes back smeared black. Bloody makeup.

'Oh, sweetie,' says Carla, in the type of caring voice that makes me want to instantly hug her. 'Let us give you a lift. Looks like you're having a tough day.' She smiles at me, and her face is just so damn *nice*.

Nancy takes my hand and I feel myself toppling over softly, like that moment a burning candle becomes more melted than solid.

'These are times I break out the emergency chocolate,' says Carla, and I laugh, even though this is the height of fridge-magnet humour.

We walk to their car, and Nancy's got her arm around me, basically holding me up. She makes us fall back from her mum a bit, and she whispers to me, 'Is everything okay?' and I nod in reflex but she goes, 'Actually really?'

I go, 'Just a headache that won't go away.'

'Oh, right,' she says.

I sniff back a bunch of cry-snot, making a disgusting noise that would probably embarrass even Titch. 'Sorry.'

'Don't worry about it,' says Nancy, and immediately I imagine her filing away this interaction as a hilarious anecdote to report to her city friends, posting it to her Facebook group *Weird Things This Psycho Country Bitch Does*. There is no way my snot sounds are going viral. Maybe they already knew about Dad. Maybe they're just looking for fresh gossip. Would they know already, though?

'You read the local paper?' I say, trying to make my voice lose its waver.

'Not really,' she says. 'It any good?'

Suddenly I'm ridiculously relieved. 'Hell no,' I say. 'Everyone loves it but there's never anything in it. It's all ads and crap. And there's this puzzle page? The crossword's called the *Chronicle Chrossword*, you know, with a 'C H' on both words, and it's so easy but people think it's super hard. My grandpa used to do it every day and he always said he was *brain training*, but they always have the same clues which is bullshit, and anyway his liver rotted away so his brain was the least of his worries.' I do a fake laugh, realising too late I'm doing nothing to dissuade Nancy I am not an emotionally challenged bogan. 'Anyway,' I say, 'don't read it.'

'Duly noted,' she says.

We get to the car and it's a brand new rental, with paper covers still on the floormats.

'The school hired it for me,' says Carla. 'I'm paranoid I'm going to back it into a tree or scratch it on something. Silly, I know.'

I smile, but I'm thinking about a car speeding past

Dad on a midnight backroad, his reflective vest fluttering in the whipped-up wind.

'You're up on the hill?' Carla says. I nod, wondering if I should just direct her to a completely different house in the neighbourhood. But, for some probably psychologically telling reason, I don't want to lie to her. I tell her the address.

The car is so quiet as we drive. I love the way the outside is sealed off. In Mum's car—or worse, Angus's ute—the world is always blaring in as hissing wind or the rumble of tyres on the road. This car is a futuristic capsule. I stare out the window and say as little as I can until we come to the street that runs off mine.

My tears have disappeared by the time we turn down the top of my driveway, and I'm feeling calm enough to think that maybe the day could improve. This is when I see the police car. Parked neatly in the driveway, clean white and blue, painfully obvious against the faded colours of our yard. There's the image of Dad in his orange prison jumpsuit, his hands gripping grimy iron bars.

'My goodness,' says Carla.

'I'm sure it's fine,' I say, too brightly, realising a few seconds later I should have said that Angus was a policeman, or we had friends who were, or any other number of reasonable explanations. My heart's hammering and I thank Carla for driving me and nearly sprint out of the car and Nancy says something to me but I don't hear it as I slam the door and run up the front steps.

I wrench open the screen door and it bashes against the cladding and I hear Mum's voice rising in the living room and I burst in ready to free Dad or throw my body in front of a bullet or lift a fridge off a baby or whatever it is you're meant to do in emergencies.

The weirdest thing, though, is that the scene just looks *normal*. Mum and Dad are on the couch and two cops are on the reclining chairs and everyone's got a mug of tea. They're all staring at me and I just freeze, like *this looks so ordinary but so* not *ordinary*.

'Hi Clancy,' says Mum. 'We're just in the middle of something at the moment.'

The cops, two guys—one younger and one older—look embarrassed.

'Is everything...okay?' I'm out of breath and there's sweat pooling in the small of my back.

'Who's this then?' says the older cop, as if I'm a three-year-old.

Dad goes, 'Just answering some questions, Clance. Nothing to worry about.' He clearly hasn't slept. His voice is high and strained.

'Where's Angus?' I say.

'He's out,' says Mum, which means she has no idea.

'Is Dad being arrested?'

Mum laughs, shaking her hands like she's trying to get water off them. 'Nothing like that!'

'We were the reporting officers at the accident,' says the younger cop, with what sounds like pride.

The older cop, who's shaved his head so no one can tell he's losing his hair—a tactic which didn't work the first time someone did it, and definitely doesn't now—says, 'Tucka'll have to come down the station and make a statement. At some stage. Sure he knows the drill.'

I go, 'The hell does *that* mean?'

'Hold on, Clance,' says Dad.

'Have they got a warrant? You need a warrant.'

The old cop holds up a hand. 'Settle down there, missy. There's no warrants here. No arrests. We're just investigating a serious accident to which your dad was a witness. We're just having a cup of tea and a chat.'

'Mister Underhill is just helping us with our enquiries,' says the younger cop.

That's what they always say on the news. *A local man is helping police with their enquiries.* Which means the local man has for dead sure done the crime and is currently down at the station getting hit with phonebooks.

Mum shoots me a look. 'Maybe you can go out for a while, Clancy.'

'I've just gotten home.'

'Clancy.' Serious teacher voice.

'How am I supposed to go anywhere without a bike?'

Mum grinds her fists into her eyes. The two cops stare into their laps. I swear the old one is grinning.

'I don't really have time for this, Clancy,' she says. She reaches over to the side table and gets her handbag. 'Get Angus and go see a movie or something.' She holds out a fifty-dollar note. A fifty. Holy shit.

'What about Titch?' I say, hoping for more.

Mum waggles her thumbs, like *he's playing video games*. 'Can you just go?' she says. 'Leave us to...talk here?'

I shrug, pocket the fifty and head for the door.

*I've been walking* maybe only five minutes when I hear a car slowing down beside me.

'Hey Pantsy,' I hear Angus shout. 'Forget something?' *Pantsy* is the name Angus gave me when he was six and I was four, and it remains one of his favourite things and, therefore, one of my least favourite. He's rolling his ute along beside me. 'Give me the fifty bucks now and we'll call it even.'

'What fifty bucks?'

'I got home just after you left. I mean, *fifty bucks*? Dad must really be in the shit.'

'Don't joke about it.'

'Life's a joke.'

I keep walking, holding my hand out behind me and raising my middle finger. I hear Angus cackling. 'Do get in,' he says in a plummy English accent. 'I shall take us to the pictures.'

'There's nothing on,' I say. 'There's never anything

on.' Barwen's cinema is just a big projector screen in the old town hall building. In the school holidays it's all kids' movies.

'Hop in anyway,' says Angus. He drives the ute up onto the kerb.

'Maniac,' I say. 'It's *my* money, though.' I get in on the passenger side, noticing a giant duffel bag in the ute's tray.

'Bullshit,' Angus says, getting back onto the road. 'That's for both of us. Mum said. You were supposed to come and get me.'

'As if you'd have come.'

'What were you going to do with the money anyway? Get a bunch of new Tegan and Sara albums?'

I punch my brother as hard as I can on his forearm.

'Shit! Settle down, Pantsy.'

'You're such a turd.'

Angus smiles and puts on a pair of reflective aviators.

I go, 'Yeah, and *I'm* the gay one.'

'Piss off. Got these in Brisbane.'

I whip them off his head and pretend to read a description written on them: 'Guaranteed not to come off while playing nude volleyball with other sweaty men. Sounds ideal.'

'I need them for driving.'

I put them on. 'They're rubbish.'

'Give 'em back.'

'Let me drive.'

'Give 'em back!'

'I'll give you ten bucks if you let me drive.'

'You haven't got your licence. You owe me twenty-five, anyway.'

'Bullshit I do.'

Angus flicks the indicator. 'I gotta get petrol.' He turns into the servo at the bottom of the hill and parks next to the bowser. 'Gimme the fifty. I need it to fill up. I'll give you change.'

'Tank's still half-full.' I tap the dash.

'I wanna top it up. The gauge's rooted anyway.'

'You'll just take the money and then not fill up.'

'As if I'd do that.'

I give him a look, like, *that's exactly what you'd do.*

He takes a deep breath and lets it out. 'All right,' he says. 'You keep the fifty, but you've got to do me a favour.'

'What's that?'

'You gotta help me out with something.' He motions to the bag in the back of the ute.

'I'm not helping you count chemtrails.'

'What?'

'Whatever it is you conspiracy theorists do.'

'It's just some surveillance. Recording data. It's like an experiment. Scientific.'

'I'm *sure* it is.'

'Just help me take some readings and write a few numbers. It'll only take a couple of hours tops.'

'Where do you do it?'

'Up the mountain.'

'Really? The Beast of Barwen?'

'Come on. It's fifty bucks.' He sticks out his hand.

'I'm not shaking your hand,' I say.

'You'll do it, though?'

'Can I drive for a bit?'

'Maybe when we get out of town.'

'I want a guarantee.'

'You in or out? I'm more than happy to leave you here at the servo and let you become a trucker's sex slave.'

'So funny. Let's just go already.'

'Awesome.' He starts up the car and swings back onto the main road, heading straight through town and out into the hills.

Secretly, I'm smiling. Fifty bucks'll buy me a new pair of shoes easy. Cheap shoes, from Spend-Less, but new shoes nonetheless. I want hi-tops or maybe rip-off Cons. Sasha—I know—will only be impressed by stilettos or thigh-high boots, but it's a start. I think about Sasha in thigh-high boots. Slinking through some cocktail party, mouth slashed with dark red lipstick, a tight black dress that wrinkles only at her hips.

Angus interrupts my thoughts with an impromptu drum solo on the steering wheel. I never want to know what awful college-rock soundtrack he's got grinding through his head at any given moment. He says, 'So Mum was pretty freaked, hey.'

'I guess. Yeah.'

'Why're you home so early? Thought you were working.'

I tell him about Raylene McCarthy and her twins, about Eloise, even about Buggs. I leave out Nancy and her mum for some reason.

'This town's full of real arseholes,' is all he says in reply.

'Cops still there when you left?'

'Yeah, just sticking around to eat all our biscuits.'

The houses thin out and we drive out through the wheat fields on a backroad that runs past the abattoir. Past the turnoff that takes you out onto the highway. It occurs to me that Dad's accident would've happened pretty close by. I wonder if there's still police tape at the scene, whether anyone has put up bouquets yet, or stuck crosses into the ground.

'You talk to Dad today?' I say.

'Nup.' Angus keeps his eyes on the road.

'He seemed better than last night.'

'Yeah. I haven't talked to him. I saw him downstairs but I couldn't—didn't know what to say.'

'You think anything'll happen to him?'

'Hard to know.'

Angus is doing his cool act. He's put a million sticks of gum in his mouth again and hasn't offered me any. With the aviators, he looks like an eighties motorcycle cop. 'Don't you care what happens to him?' I say.

Angus shakes his head. 'He'll get what he deserves, I guess.'

'What if he goes to jail?' Voice at full Disney princess.

'You don't know what it's like,' he says.

'What *what's* like?'

Angus sighs. 'To be constantly called a fuck-up. That's all Dad ever does. Reels off the ways he thinks I've gone wrong, the decisions I could've made better. As if his life's been perfect. As if he's ever made it easy for me. This is just karma.'

'He can get pissed off sometimes, but—'

'You don't know, cause you're the smart one. It's like, they don't have to worry about how you're going to turn out because you'll be a scientist or a lawyer or whatever. With me, with Dad, it's like it's his life's purpose to have a go at me.'

'I don't think he's *that* bad. Is he?' Dad *is* a dick to Angus, but Angus is a dick back. And, really, my brother never settles on one thing long enough to fail or succeed. He always just changes his mind.

'You've got no idea,' he says. 'Uni was the worst. Having to come back home was totally humiliating.'

'You didn't have to come back.'

'Yeah, I did. Head lecturer had it in for me, just because I had the balls to ask the tough questions. Just cause I wasn't a sheep like the rest of them.'

I knew exactly the types of questions Angus would've asked. He's always been a *contrarian*: this is the word Dad uses. Constantly trying to find ways to undermine authority, to take the opposite view to what he's being shown is right. He would have spouted half-baked conspiracies all the way through his business degree, about the World Bank or the Illuminati or alien cover-ups: any of a number of obsessively insane theories he's crammed into his head at the expense of basic life skills.

'Rather be a sheep than a loon,' I say under my breath.

We drive for about forty minutes, coming way up into the hills, following the spiral road that circles partway up Mount Meyer. On the other side is the national park and between, over the crest of the mountain, is thick bushland that gradually grades up into cool air and a kind of half-rainforest.

Angus swings off the main road and plunges us down a dirt track with a sign that tells me it's a firebreak. The canopy of trees closes tighter and tighter above us and after a couple of minutes Angus pulls the ute to the side of the road and kills the engine. It's only after we stop that I remember I wanted to drive part of the way. I remind myself to nag Angus about it on the way back.

'This is it,' he says.

'I'm not going to have to walk through mud am I?' I peer out at the dark foliage lining the track.

'Nah, it's cool. You can walk it fine in sneakers or whatever.'

'Can I walk it in my *only* pair of shoes?'

'Absolutely,' he says, hopping out of the car.

I get out, surprised by how cold the air is. Something flies at my face, smothering it, and I scrabble to get it off.

'It's a jumper,' says Angus, 'you pussy. Temperature drop.'

'You could've just *handed* it to me.' It's some scratchy army surplus thing, but I put it on.

'Not out here. We're adventuring now.'

I roll my eyes. 'How often do you drink your own urine when you're up here *adventuring*? More than at home, or the same amount?'

A backpack hits me in the head.

When we're all strapped in, Angus plunges off the track at a seemingly random point.

'Jesus. Wait!' I'm worried at how dark it'll be in the bush, and how my legs will most likely come out covered in leeches.

'There's a track just through here,' says Angus from somewhere behind what I'm sure is a fatally poisonous tree.

I follow his voice through the thicket and sure enough it opens up a bit and there's a faint track winding through the bush. It's slightly lighter, somehow, too, like we've just gone through the forest's front hall and are now in the living room. The sun is a glimmer in the tops of the gum trees.

'Nice,' I say involuntarily.

'I know, right? Come on, just up this way.' Angus ducks under a branch and skips up the track. He's got a silver box in his hand. It's got a little handle and it looks a bit like a tape player.

'What's that you're carrying?'

'Digital recorder. For audio.'

'Course it is.' I start to wonder what's hidden in my backpack. A taser? Half a gram of coke? My brother could be up to anything out here.

The track takes us up a hill and there's spiky grass that cuts into my shins. 'Are there snakes here?' I say.

'No snakes,' says Angus over his shoulder. 'All the scorpions scare them away.'

We get to the crest of the hill and Angus stops. He holds his arm out so I can't walk past him.

'Why'd you stop?'

'Shh.' Angus puts his finger up to his lips.

'What?'

'D'you hear that?' Angus's eyes are shifting wildly, trying to catch something up in the canopy.

'What?'

'If you listen *really* closely...' There's a pause, then he rips a huge fart.

'Gross!' I say, screwing up my face. 'That sounded solid.'

He giggles like an idiot. 'If a man farts in the forest and no one's around to hear it...' then he's laughing too hard to talk.

'Really mature,' I say. 'This all you do out here? Just shart and play explorers?'

Angus is still laughing. 'You wouldn't know a joke if it bit you on the arse.'

'Let's keep moving then, before something *does* bite me on the arse.'

Angus points down to a clearing at the bottom of the slope. 'It's just down there.'

I can't see anything special at first but when we get down there I notice there's sort of a crude hideout covered in sticks and leaves, teepee-shaped and really not at all camouflaged.

'This is the base of my operations,' says Angus. 'Have a look inside.'

I take off my backpack. Up close, I see that underneath the covering it's a tent. I unzip the entrance and poke my head inside. The floor's covered with a blue tarp, and there's plastic tubs stacked up everywhere. I lift the lid on one. It's got a bunch of exercise books in it and a torch. Angus's sleeping bag is rolled up in one corner. There's a strip of hessian taped to one wall and when I pull it up I realise Angus has cut a hole where you can peer through and see the clearing.

Angus crawls into the space. There's hardly room for both of us. 'Pretty cool, huh?'

'Are girls even allowed in your special fort?'

Angus ignores me, pulling his backpack and tape player in behind him. 'Check this out.' He pulls a black contraption out of the pack and unfolds it. It's a tripod, which he sets up beneath the hole in the wall. Then a camera, which he fixes onto the tripod.

'Where'd you get that from? Looks expensive.'

'Bought it.' He sticks a cord in from the digital recorder to the camera.

'With what?'

Angus switches on the camera and it makes a little whirring noise. 'Money.'

'What money?'

'I need you to go outside and help me test this.'

'What money, Angus?' Why the hell is he arguing with me over twenty-five bucks when he's got the dough to buy cameras and tripods and audio recorders?

Angus flips a little screen out from the side of the camera and I can see the clearing in miniature. 'From Grandpa,' he says.

'The money Grandpa left us? That's in the bank.'

'*Was* in the bank. There's still some there.'

'But that was for uni, or investment or whatever.'

'I'm not *going* to uni. This *is* my investment. I'm eighteen so I can do what I want with it.'

'And you spent it chasing made-up monsters?' I make a dismissive sound with my mouth that horrifies me because it sounds just like Mum.

'The Beast of Barwen is well-documented,' he says, like he's reading from a script. 'I've done a lot of research. This is where it should be. No one's going to say it's made up when I get proper photographic evidence.'

'And what if, for instance, you don't find the beast?'

'I will.'

'Uh-huh.'

'Do you want to keep arguing with me, or do you want to help me test the audio so we can get back to town?'

'It's your money.' I clamber outside. 'What do you want me to do?'

'Go to the edge of the clearing and walk past the hideout,' says Angus from inside the tent. 'Make some noise while you're doing it.'

'What sort of noise?'

'Just some sounds. Loud and soft. I want to see what I can pick up.'

I backtrack to a nearby tree and walk forward like a zombie, arms held out in front of me. I go, 'AAAAHM THE BEEEAST OF BAAAAAHRWENNN. AAAAHM GONNA WALK IN FRONT OF THIS NATURAL LOOKING PILE OF STICKS WITH A CAAAAHMERA POINTING OUT OF IT.'

'Very funny,' says Angus's muffled voice. 'Keep going.'

'NOBODY'S EEEEEEHVER SEEEEN ME, WHICH IS WEEEEEIRD BECAUSE I'M AAAAHLWAYS WALKING AROUND SAAAAHYING MY NAAAAME. AAAAHM THE BEEEST OF BAAAAAHRWENNN!' I'm past the hideout now, so I turn back around. 'Why is the beast going to walk through this clearing, anyway?' I say.

'Look in your backpack,' says Angus.

'My backpack?'

'Open it.'

I do as I'm told. I open it and pull out a heavy black bin bag. It unrolls in my hand, and the sound it makes is not pleasant.

'What's in here?'

'Open it.'

I untie the handles and look inside. Two eyes stare back at me. It's a pig's head, its mouth gaping open. I scream.

I hear Angus choking and gasping with laughter.

'What the *fuck*?' I go to kick the bag away from me but I don't want to touch it. 'You *psycho*!'

Angus comes out of the hideout and picks up the bag. 'How am I supposed to catch a beast without bait?'

'You fucking psycho. You killed a *pig* for this?'

'You can get heads from the abattoir for basically nothing.'

'I want to go home.' All I can think about is the pig's rheumy little death-eyes.

'Just let me set it up and we can get out of here. Great audio, by the way. Crystal clear.'

'Don't expect me to ever come out here again.'

'Ah, you love it,' he says. He produces a bunch of tent pegs and a mallet from his bag. 'Want to help me tie it down?'

When we get back everyone's already in bed and the house is all switched off. Angus asks me if I want to get Macca's and I'm starving but I've had more than enough of his company for one day. He drives off and I root through the fridge for any evidence of dinner. Mum's foul tuna mornay from a few days ago is sitting under Glad Wrap on the bottom shelf. All that's left in the bread bin is a razor-thin crust sitting alone in a knotted bag. Bloody hell.

I head out the back to the chest freezer where there are usually a few squashed loaves of Home Brand if you dig deep enough. I mentally prepare myself for whatever other animal parts Angus has stashed away.

Luckily, it's so frosted over inside that even if a whole pig was in there I wouldn't be able to see it. I break off a few chunks of ice but don't find any bread, even when I lean my whole body in. Then, frozen over in the very bottom corner, is a pack of Cornettos. I yank the packet from the ice and peer inside. There's four left. *Yes.* Forget the Beast of Barwen: this is a real discovery. Uneaten ice-creams just don't exist in the Underhill household.

I'm about to go back inside and smuggle my discovery upstairs when I notice there's light coming from the window in the shed. I feel relief, then guilt, when I realise I've forgotten about Dad's visit to the police station. Fifty bucks and a severed animal head. This is all it takes, apparently, to make me not worry about my dad going to jail.

I walk over the wet grass in my bare feet and knock on the shed door.

'Yeah?' Dad sounds tired. There's a soft murmur of something behind the door.

'It's Clancy.'

'Oh. G'night then, Clance.'

'I wanted to check you're okay.'

'I'm all good. G'night.'

'I've got Cornettos.'

I hear a chair scrape. 'What kind?'

I check the box. 'Nuts and shit. Whatever that type is you like.'

The garage door rumbles open. Dad's wearing his Broncos jersey. 'Where'd you find those?'

'Deep freeze.'

'Nice work.'

'I saw the mornay. Couldn't do it.'

Dad grimaces, like, *I know*. He says, 'I'm listening to the cricket.'

'Want to split these?' I hold up the packet. 'Two each.'

'What time is it?'

'School holidays is what time it is.'

Dad pretends to think for a moment before throwing his thumb over his shoulder. 'Go on, then.'

I smile. Dad used to give me rides in the back of his ute when I was little, before they invented Workplace Health and Safety. He foolishly did it once, driving me around a bumpy paddock, and I loved it so much I'd pester him constantly about it. When he'd eventually give in it felt like the highlight of my life. He'd do the same movement: thumb over the shoulder: *Go on, then.*

I take out two Cornettos and Dad pulls the rollerdoor back down. He's got both windows open with flyscreen covers so the mozzies don't get in. His old radio is propped up on his workbench and there's an esky next to his chair. He drags out a bucket seat from behind the bench for me and I sit down in it and it smells like motor oil.

'What cricket is it?' I say.

'Australia India. Mumbai. First test.'

'Just start today?'

Dad nods.

'How're we doing?'

Dad shrugs and turns up the volume. 'Pretty crap. Dead track, and we can't play spin for shit. We're already four down for eighty-odd.'

I unwrap my Cornetto and except for a bit of freezer burn it's fantastic. 'We'll come back,' I say.

'Maybe.'

I like cricket. More watching it than listening to it usually. I used to like the summers when there was a test match and the TV was on all day. Mum would let us put cold flannels on our heads or stick our feet in ice water and we were allowed to keep the fan on as long as we wanted. All of us, even Mum, sitting together. Dad was a good cricketer before his back went. He opened the bowling for Barwen's second team and went to state championships with the firsts one year.

Dad takes a Cornetto and puts the other two into the esky. He picks his green heat pack off the arm of the chair and puts it behind his back. We listen to the cricket for a while, the commentators talking about the pitch for ten minutes. Australia doesn't lose any wickets, but nearly every ball you can hear the players and the crowd appealing for something.

Dad opens the esky and gets a beer out. He throws me another Cornetto. 'You have the rest if you like. If you didn't have dinner.'

'Thanks.' I fill my face with more ice-cream. 'So, were you okay today?'

Dad swigs his beer. 'Was I *okay*?'

'With the…with the cops.'

'Just doing their job.'

'Did you have to go down to the station?'

'I gave a statement.'

'What about Mum?'

Dad leans forward to remove the heat pack, tossing it

on the ground. 'Bloody thing never stays warm.'

'Did you have to have a lawyer?'

Dad turns to me. 'Just trying to listen to the score here,' he says.

'Sorry.'

He rubs his eyes. 'Nah, mate, I'm sorry. It's just been...a busy couple of days.' His elbow slips off the armrest and it's only then I wonder how many beers he's already had. 'Your mother, she just *worries* so much. Makes it so much worse than it already is. She's always been like that.'

Behind where Dad's sitting is a pinboard with photos of us all. They're old pictures, all that same faded colour photos get when they're exposed to the air, so you can't tell when they were taken unless you know the people in them. The one of Mum and Dad's wedding day could've been taken at the same time as the one of me sitting in a laundry tub with a sieve on my head. The one with us in front of Sydney Opera House when Mum's hair is a big perm and I've got gel bracelets all up one arm. The one of Angus playing guitar with dad's sunglasses on: aviators, too big for his face. There's albums of Dad's photos somewhere, too. He used to take them out all the time for me to look at. Dad in jeans and a leather jacket, leaning on his motorbike. His hair dark and thick.

'What did you have to do,' I say, 'at the station?'

'Just had to tell them what happened.'

I nod. There's so many questions I want to ask him. 'Hopefully it didn't take too long, though.'

'It was long enough.' Dad shifts in his chair. He takes a long swig of beer. 'They make…they make you go through it time after time after time. Three seconds out of my life.'

'I guess they have to be thorough, or whatever.'

'Even after,' he says, 'when I was in the back of the ambulance with a blanket over my shoulders, the cops are there trying to trip me up with questions. Nothing changes.' Dad clenches his jaw. 'Ah, I'm too tired, Clance. Don't listen to me.'

'It must've been awful,' I say quietly.

There's a roar of noise through the radio. Another wicket down.

The next few days I kick around the house, and there's this sort of stillness. It's not unusual that none of us are talking to each other, but this time it feels like we *should* be, and all the unspoken words are clogging up the air around us. Even Titch—I don't know how much he's been told—seems to know he has to be on his best behaviour. Mum's even more distracted than usual, so he just plays video games all hours of the day. Mum goes out shopping and comes back with IGA bags, meaning she's driven out of town instead of going to the Coles in Barwen.

The phone's off the hook because some reporter from Brisbane got our number and Titch answered when she called. Mum ripped out the cord and she was still shaking half an hour later. Kept saying, 'Vultures,' over and over. A news van came up to the top of the driveway one afternoon, a satellite dish poking out conspicuously from its roof. I was up in my room and I saw it creep up, stay for a moment, then drive away. Dad sleeps most of the day, goes out to the shed late in the afternoon and stays there until late at night to listen to the cricket. Angus is out most of the time. Probably up in the mountains or out at the observatory, who knows.

In the mornings I collect the paper and take it up to my room. Dad's name is in there now, going from 'a local man' to 'council worker Robert Underhill'. They're still not calling him a suspect, because they can't, but it's clear the town's already made up its mind. Yesterday morning there was more graffiti, and again Mum and I scrubbed it off. The front of the house is slowly turning pink. Dad's not had to go back to the police station, but I know he's been suspended from work. *Investigation Pending, Court Dates, Legal Fees.* These are the snatches of conversation I hear. I spend nights awake, thinking about Dad sitting in the back of an ambulance with a ring of cops around him, thinking about the pig's head and its creamy white eyes, thinking about Buggs and Sasha driving past our house every night with empty spray cans on the back seat.

It's the fourth, maybe fifth day after the accident and I can't take it any more. I can't focus on music or books or TV. I'm being driven crazy with my own thoughts.

I check my watch. I can still make it. Dad's still asleep, and Mum's taken a day's tutoring a few towns over so there's no one to ask questions as I stash a muesli bar in my pocket and head out to the shed, wrench up the door and drag out Angus's old bike. He hasn't used it in a year.

It's covered with dust and cobwebs. I get the bike pump and miraculously the flat tyres don't have any punctures. The brakes seem to work. I spend a little while cleaning it up and soon it's good to go.

It feels so much better to be outside again. I don't know why I haven't thought of using Angus's bike before. I used to be so jealous of him on this bike with its gears and proper grips. I ride up onto the main road and coast down the hill slowly, enjoying the wind in my face. Swing left just before the servo and climb up the small rise. No problems. I stop for a moment at the top and let the wind buffet my face. Okay, I think. I'm going to do it.

All morning I've thought about Nature Club. I haven't missed one all year, and today was going to be the first time. I've gone back and forth thinking about it. Would everyone ignore me? Would George Parry tell me to go home? Would Nancy still want to hang out? Nancy. I feel bad about running out of the car when her and her mum gave me that lift. They were so nice to me, and I didn't even say thank you. There's no way they'll be nice to me now. They'll know about Dad. But I just can't spend another day indoors.

By the time I get to Landsdowne my lungs and legs are burning. Even with the seat all the way down, the pedals are slightly out of reach, and I miss the gears a couple of times. Still, no more *Lightning Lady*. I check my watch and I'm only just late. I'm used to throwing my bike on the ground but Angus's has a kickstand, so I leave the bike upright by the gate. It'll be just my luck if it gets stolen. Then again, it'd serve Angus right.

George Parry's office is empty. I hurry up to the water tank, hoping I haven't missed too much. There's no one at the tank but I can see shadows in the greenhouse. My heart starts pumping again as I push back the plastic tarp door.

Everyone's there, bent over a row of seedlings. My feet crunch on the gravel and suddenly everyone looks up. I focus on Nancy immediately, her surprised smile seeming to appear before the rest of her. George Parry, somehow, is so involved in whatever he's doing that he doesn't look up.

'Hey Clancy,' Nancy says too fast. 'We're measuring seed vigour, then we get to do random sampling in the bush. In quadrants.'

'It's actually pronounced *quadrats*,' says Glenn, any personal prejudice against me overridden by his need to be the most pedantic person in the room.

'You'll know some of this, Clancy,' says Mr P without looking up, 'but I don't have time to start again.' His voice is flatter than usual, the tone he usually reserves for when DD knocks something over during an experiment.

I hurry over to the group and Nancy shuffles over to make room for me. 'Thanks,' I say.

Mr P keeps working, hunched over a segmented wooden box filled with different seeds, telling us what he's doing, what we should be recording, but I'm too busy watching everyone else.

'Now you can try it yourselves,' says George Parry. 'If you go in pairs you can find a plot and start your measurements.'

Nancy grabs my hand and pulls me towards her. I smell perfume. 'We'll go together,' she says. 'Come on.' She leads me down the other end of the greenhouse, and when we're out of earshot of the others, turns to me, her eyes wide. 'I'm so glad you came,' she says.

'I had to take my brother's bike,' I say, then wonder why this is something she needs to know.

'I had no idea about the...about your dad. I didn't know the *family stuff* was that. I'm really sorry.'

'That's...fine.' She's apologising to me? This isn't right. I feel the urge to cry and laugh at the same time.

'It must be horrible.'

'I'm sorry I didn't thank you and your mum,' I say. 'For the lift home.'

'Oh, that's fine. Was everything okay? With the police?' She lowers her voice to a whisper.

'Yeah, everything's...' Everything's what? Okay? Horrible? The same as ever? I push my finger into a seedling container, keep pushing until I can feel the bottom. 'It'll be okay.' I try on a smile and my lips feel like they're cracking open.

'Well, if you need to talk to anyone...'

I dig my finger around in the dirt, wishing I could follow it down to the centre of the earth and stay there. Why is it making me feel so sad that someone's being nice to me? I grit my teeth but the tears start to come out. My head's shivering as I'm trying to keep them in and then my whole body's shaking.

Nancy almost pushes me through the plastic flap and back out into the open air, moments before I break down, howling like a freak and I can't stop it because she's rubbing my back and somehow this just makes it worse.

**When I look** up, when I think it's safe to open my eyes again, Nancy's wearing sunglasses. We're sitting under a tree and my whole body feels emptied out.

'Wow,' I say. 'I'm so sorry you had to see that.'

She shakes her head. 'It's good to let it out.'

I peer up through the branches of the tree and the sunlight scatters everywhere. I feel really, really lost. I've never cried like this in front of anyone, let alone someone I don't know. 'Yeah,' I say. 'I guess.'

'We can stay here for as long as you need.'

I sit up and try to surreptitiously deal with all the horrendous fluids leaking from my face.

'I'm glad you came today,' says Nancy. 'I mean, it's fun, but Glenn keeps staring at me.'

'It's so rare for him to see a girl he didn't download.'

Nancy laughs. 'This is why it's better when you're here.' She leans back. 'It's cool, though. Nature Club. I never had anything like this in Brisbane.'

'It's *cool*?'

'You've got no idea. I feel like some of the people at my old school had never seen a tree.'

I hold my eyes open like they need air as well. 'Yeah, well I do like it. I guess that's sort of lame.'

'Why?'

'I just, you know, look around sometimes and think *Do I come here just to feel comfortable*?'

'What do you mean?'

'I make fun of Glenn and the rest of them, but at the same time I still think I'm not as happy as they are. I don't even fit in with the misfits.'

'Why don't you think you fit in?' Nancy is holding a leaf. She's torn it up carefully so that only the central vein is left behind.

'It doesn't matter. I'm just crapping on.'

'No, it makes perfect...I get it, totally.' She spins the leaf spine between her fingers.

I go, 'It's just my default setting, I guess. Feeling like I'm going in one direction while everyone else is going the other.'

Nancy doesn't say anything, just pushes the sunglasses up onto her head. There's a Chanel logo on the side, giant, so you won't miss it. Her blouse has lace swirling all through it in delicate, repeating patterns. It's amazingly nice and I know I'll never own anything like it. Everything about her is so shiny and perfect and what is she even doing here? She doesn't even realise she can do so much better. I notice I'm picking at the sole of my shoe where the glue has come off and whip my hand away like I've been burnt.

'You okay?' Nancy's face has a look of soap opera concern.

'Fine. Just allergies.' This, of course, makes no sense. I squint my eyes up at the greenhouse, hoping that Mr P will come out and tell us to get back to the experiment. There's no movement from the door.

Nancy clears her throat. 'Do you, um, do you not have many friends here?'

'What?'

'In Barwen. It feels like, maybe, it's hard to make... real friends somewhere like this.' She shrugs, her shiny hair shaking and I think of Mum steepling her fingers at the dinner table, hoping to *have a chat, just us girls.*

'What do you know about it?' I say.

'I just...I don't know.'

Why am I even talking to her about this stuff? Someone I've only known for five minutes. Something in my stomach turns over. 'You don't know anything about me,' I say. I hear the cop laughing at Dad, saying, *sure he knows the drill.*

'No need to be defensive,' says Nancy. 'I'm just trying to be nice.' Her face is all scrunched up like, *it's not my fault you're a crazy bitch.*

'Yeah well thanks for trying to be my friend, but I'm just fine, actually.'

'Which is why you're still crying. Clancy, I—'

I dig my nails into my palms. 'Don't pretend like you know me. You come here thinking you're better than everyone just because you're this *amazing* person from the city.'

'I never said that.'

'You find this country freak you can buddy up to just so you get a good story for your friends.' There's kind of a warning signal going off in my head but also a louder angry drone that has built up for so long I can no longer deny it. 'Everyone thinks I'm this fucked-up weirdo with no friends who can't talk to people or have *relationships* just because I don't want to dress up like a slut and give out handjobs every day.'

'Clancy, I—'

I'm still talking, and it's all coming out. 'I don't get my self-worth from getting attention and I don't go to parties because I don't get them and somehow it's my fault that I can't do all this stuff. Everyone's expected to like the same things and enjoy dancing and getting your eyelashes curled and being so fucking happy about it all.'

Nancy holds up her hands like someone in a reality show. 'Forget it,' she says. 'Sorry I took an interest.'

'You *took an interest*? Sorry I wasn't a good enough hobby for you.'

'Jesus. No need to be a bitch about it, just because you're going through some stuff.'

'You don't know shit about what I'm going through.

109

Fuck you and your fucking sunglasses.' I jump up and the sole on my stupid shoe bends back and nearly trips me over. 'Fucking hell!' I kick the ground over and over and over until my big toe stings and I've started crying again.

I look back at the tree and Nancy's gone. A noisy miner breaks the air above me, shaking a branch as it takes off. My face burns. I can actually feel my pulse high up in my cheekbones and I hate the world just a little bit more, just that extra sour amount. Nancy will have gone back to the greenhouse and when someone asks *where's Clancy?* she'll just twirl her finger at the side of her head, like *bitch be crazy* and everyone will laugh and I'll never be able to come back to Nature Club ever again.

And part of me knows I've been the world's biggest idiot, getting angry at Nancy when she's done practically nothing wrong. But, really, what is everyone's obsession with knowing everything about me? Why can't people just mind their own bloody business?

I hobble off towards the front gate because I've probably broken my toe. This is good, I think. I'll just go home, go to my room, and never come out. I'll order pizzas and get them slid under the door. I'll read books and sleep and listen to music until I die of boredom and then the coroner can examine my body and talk into her little tape recorder and say *what a fucking freak. Glad I didn't have to know her.*

*Every time I* pedal harder I hear my breath huffing in my ears. I'm not going home. I need to be nowhere. I need to have no one around me. I need space. As I come back into town I skip the skate park, loop around behind it and follow the river until it disappears through the weir and back into the bush. I come up past the tennis courts and follow the road that leads to the hospital, turning off onto the highway at the last minute. Flying down the slope, wanting to lose control.

I hear the scream of a semi-trailer behind me and try to ignore it. Fuck this particular trucker. Then he blares his horn and I instinctively swerve onto the road's shoulder and the second after I feel a rush of wind as the truck passes, kicking up dust and diesel and the smell of livestock. I watch the back of the trailer and the cloud swirls back at me and I get a big lungful of dust and grit all in my eyes. I cane the footbrakes and my toe hammers out a big bolt of pain.

I half-fall off the bike and double over coughing, grasping for Angus's old sports bottle that's clipped to the frame. I squirt it in my scrunched-up eyes and down my throat. It's lukewarm and tastes of plastic and it's absolutely disgusting. Eventually my breathing gets back to normal and I throw the bottle away. I'm covered in red smears of dirt and my throat feels like an industrial rubbish chute. As the dust clears a familiar shape emerges in the distance. The tall shape of the observatory. I wheel the bike over and lean it against the metal base of the tower.

I just need a moment to myself. A moment to think things over. The sun has lost its sting now it's late afternoon, so I decide to climb to the top.

As I'm going up the steps, I fantasise—for the millionth time in my life—about when I have a car and I can escape whenever I want. Properly escape. I've saved all my money from work, and once I turn eighteen I'll get my share of Grandpa's money as well. With a car, in the time it took me to cycle out here, I could be in a completely different town. I could be a stranger sitting in a cafe, walking a new main street. I could be whoever I want to be.

I get to the top of the observatory and the echoes of my footsteps on the metal fade away and I can't see any stars but I can see the hazy hills on the horizon and the wheat fields and the tip of Barwen Presbyterian poking up above the rest of the town. I realise I've never actually been up here. It's always been the domain of Angus, and therefore a place not worth worrying about, but the the truth is, it's actually pretty impressive. Relatively speaking.

'Wow,' I say to no one in particular. Then I say it again. And again. It's just me and the open air so I say it again, louder. And then I shout it. My voice empties into all that space and it feels really, really good. I open out my arms like in the movies and scream as loud as I can and I feel tears pricking at my eyes, like *why have I never done this before?*

Then I see the speck of a car coming over the hill and I quickly lean back on the rail so it looks like I'm just resting there or whatever and not shouting like a lunatic. The car gets closer and it's like a bad dream because it's a brown Monaro. It gets closer and there's the polaroid windscreen and I'm thinking shit shit shit cause I'm up here like a sitting duck and the car's slowing down and no he must have seen me and can't I have one nice moment in my life without it being ruined the very next second?

The Monaro goes past slowly and I will it to keep going but it stops twenty metres ahead and I wish that I'd spent some of my car money on a phone—even the fifty in my pocket might have bought me a really shitty one—and I could call the police *right now.* I grip the warm metal of the railing as the car reverses back towards me. I try to calculate the distance to the ground, whether I could somehow land safely and jump on the bike and escape.

The car door opens before I can think of anything else but instead of Buggs unfolding himself it's Sasha. She's in a black T-shirt and blue cutoffs and my fear is replaced by something else entirely.

First thought: why isn't she wearing black jeans like she always does? Second thought: what the hell am *I* wearing? I don't know the answer to the first question but the second one is easy: an old singlet that used to belong to Angus that says *Porky's Bar & Grill* on the front, footy shorts and my eternally daggy boots with their soles flapping off.

Bloody hell. The back of the singlet, I now remember, has a drawing of a pig with a monocle and top hat holding a knife and fork, licking its lips. I never thought about whether the pig knew it was about to become a cannibal or not. Either way, pigs are out to get me this week.

'Hey!' Sasha calls up.

My throat dries up. This is only the second time she's ever spoken to me. The first time was at the supermarket when I was staring at a Toblerone trying to talk myself out of buying it and blocking the checkout and she said *Are you going to buy it or hypnotise it?* and I didn't realise it was her until she went past me and her perfume was amazing and who spends so long analysing a chocolate bar anyway?

'Hey, hello?' She thinks I haven't heard her.

I peer over the edge.

Sasha waves to me. Sasha Strickland waves to me.

I wave back and somehow croak out, 'Hi.'

'I saw you up there as I was driving past.'

'Right.' I laugh, like we're making sparkling conversation.

She squints up into the sun and her nose crinkles at the top. 'Just wanted to say I'm sorry to hear about your dad and that.'

'Oh. Thanks.' Some small part of my brain tells me that she's lying, that she's got something to do with the spray-paint and the cops and all the rest but the big part of my brain tells the small part to shut the hell up.

'Do you want to come down for a sec?' she says. 'I'd come up, but...' she points to her strappy sandals.

I stare at her legs for a second too long. 'Sure,' I say, and make my way back down the stairs in a way that says *I'm invited down from the tops of observatories all the time* but also *don't leave don't leave stay right there don't move.*

*It's like a* dream and I'm sure it *is* a dream when Sasha asks me if I want to go for a milkshake. It's a fifties dream, maybe. Malted milks and polka-dot dresses.

'There's this place I go to out on the highway. The roadhouse?'

'Yeah.'

'It's, like, super scummy but they do these milkshakes that are, like, *incredible*.' Her eyes open wide when she says *incredible* and she's got these blue eyes like *how blue can I possibly be*?

'You got anything you need to bring, or...'

I glance back quickly at Angus's bike and shake my head. He never uses it anyway. Besides, who's going to steal such a shitty-looking bike?

'Cool,' she says. 'Get in. Sorry about the mess.'

I open the passenger door and it's a weird feeling because it's Buggs's car, but at the same time it's the place I've imagined being inside so many times, down at the skate park, Sasha changing out of her work clothes and into her black jeans. The Monaro's interior is not how I've imagined it. I pictured a gleaming chrome dashboard that Sasha checked her lipstick in, dark panelled wood that ate the light. In reality, it's a normal looking car. The floor on the passenger side has sand on it and a Chupa-Chup stuck to the carpet. A couple of tissues stick out of the glovebox.

I steal a glance at Sasha's cheek. She puts on enormous sunglasses, which I now immediately want a pair of. They're not Chanel. They're too cool for that. The passenger seat isn't lowered like the drivers seat, which is a bit weird. She pulls out onto the highway.

'So everyone's being shit to you, right?'

'Sorry?' I pull on my seatbelt.

'Cause of your dad's thing. Like, no one's going to the makeup place.'

'Oh, you know. It's just some people.'

'I knew that girl who got killed, Cassie. A real princess. You know her parents are like *super* rich?'

'I didn't know that.' I'm beginning to feel a little sick in my stomach. Sasha is a really bad driver and the souped-up engine lurches the car every time she changes gears.

'Like, she was a year below me? And she was always getting special treatment when she sat in on our classes. She was going to graduate early but she didn't.'

'It's pretty sad.'

'Yeah I guess. And the other guy was, like, Buggs's second cousin through marriage or something? They never did anything together or anything like that. They didn't hang out.'

Sasha speaks really fast and the engine keeps whining so I can't understand all of what she says.

'Piece of shit!' Sasha hits the steering wheel. 'Like, why can't this just be a *normal* car? You drive?'

'No. Not yet.'

'It's a pain in the arse. Cars are so expensive. Like, Buggs and his dad fix them or whatever? But if I had to pay for it, it would be, like, *super* expensive. You smoke?'

'Yeah. Um, sometimes,' says the Disney princess.

Sasha tries to wrestle a pack of cigarettes from a pocket in her shorts but can't quite manage it. 'Can you get 'em out for me?' She keeps flitting her eyes between the cigarettes and the road.

*Shit shit shit.* 'Sure.' I reach over and try to get the packet out without touching her.

'Lighter's in there as well. Help yourself.'

'O-okay.' I fish out the cigarettes with my thumb and forefinger, being super careful to just touch the packet. But I can't get it out without feeling her leg through the pocket. I feel like I'm about to pass out, but then I get the packet free, a hairband wrapped around it holding the lighter in place.

I haven't smoked since Angus's going-away party at the start of the year. I light one up and hand it to Sasha, who takes a huge drag. I try to light one for myself but for some reason my hands are shaking and the lighter won't fire a second time. Eventually I get it to work and I wind the window down so I can take tiny kid-puffs without Sasha noticing.

We get to the roadhouse and Sasha doesn't slow down as she swings into the carpark. She parks at an angle over two spots. 'Honestly, I drive like an Asian sometimes.' She laughs, and it's beautiful, and I laugh as well despite the joke not really being a joke. 'Buggs hates me driving his car, but fuck him, you know?'

We get out of the car and I'm feeling sort of seasick even though we're nowhere near the ocean. Everything's going in super-speed, but I keep telling myself this is what I want, this is what I want. Maybe this is something finally going right, to balance out all the shitty stuff. Friends with Sasha Strickland, this is my reward.

Inside the roadhouse it's ice-cold. You can hear the air-conditioning roaring even before you go through the sliding doors. They only built it a few years ago and it's designed for big trucks stopping on their way up or down the coast between Brisbane and Sydney. The parking bay is enormous, and there's a whole football field of bitumen which is just for trucks to turn around in. When it first opened everyone in town went here even though it sells the same shit food as any other servo, just from inside a bigger building.

We go up to the counter and Sasha leans over so only her toes touch the ground. There's a tiny strip of skin between her shirt and her shorts, perfectly white. Her legs are much longer and a better shape than mine will ever be.

A guy comes to the counter and I realise it's Troy McCarthy, the guy I used to skate with. Son of Raylene, the shingle-skinned face of Barwen's Underhill Hate Campaign. 'Hi there,' he says, not—understandably— looking at me, but at Sasha. 'What can I get you?' Troy's face hasn't really changed from how I remember it: his features have just grown outwards with his face. He has his mum's tiny eyes, but on him they're kinder.

'Two malt shakes, please. What flavour d'ya want, *Clancy*?' My name, her voice. 'Caramel's the best.'

'Caramel's great,' I say. Troy looks at me and sort of smiles. I go to say *hi* but it gets caught in my throat and he's already turned away by the time I go to say it again.

We're sitting there with matching milkshakes, Sasha and me. Somehow, things aren't going like I always thought they would. Firstly, she invited me, when in fact our first date was meant to be the result of a concerted campaign I'd waged to convince her of my attractiveness/ worth. Secondly, we're sitting face to face under twenty-four-hour fluorescents, with the unromantic buzz of air-con in our ears and endless flabby wedges of seated trucker's arsecrack as our view.

I've often walked past Sasha's mum's travel agency, where she works, even though I never went in. Hoping for a quick glimpse as I went past, a fleeting view of her profile: white blouse, blue scarf, spidery telephone headset.

Now I have her all to myself it's almost too much. There's no more mystery.

I've never thought about what her voice would really sound like, or how she'd have a tiny pimple beside her nose or how she'd spin a milkshake container a quarter-turn every few seconds like if she didn't it would disappear.

But then she smiles, and I go all warm, and I forget any doubts that this is the right thing to be doing.

'So you've been here all your life?' she says.

'In Barwen?'

'Yeah.'

'You're, like, part-Aboriginal though, right?'

This takes me by surprise. 'Uh, like, an eighth or a sixteenth or something. I guess. Mum's dad's dad was or something.'

'Just...your skin.'

I look down at my arm. Yellowy-brown, made blotchy under roadhouse lights. Me and Angus and Titch have all got it, and it just looks like we're dirty or sick. Neither one thing or the other, the same as the rest of me, halfway between *nothing much* and *what the hell?*

'What's your, like, tribe or whatever?'

I shrug like I don't know, but I've got a bookmark at home that Mum gave me ages ago with a dot painting on it and the word *Bundjalung*. Just another confusion. No one ever asks about it, though. It's kind of cool that Sasha does.

'I'm, like, so white,' she says. 'I wish I was more interesting.'

'You're pretty interesting,' I say.

'Yeah, right.' She examines her own arm. 'But your dad, though,' she says. 'Shit, right? How's he taking it?'

'He's okay. Mum's worse.' I decide to try something.

'Someone spray-painted our house.'

'What, like graffiti?'

'Yeah. About my dad. And like a skull and crossbones.'

'Fuck, that's heavy. Some people are shit.' She seems genuinely concerned, but surely she'd know what Buggs gets up to? Maybe not. Maybe it wasn't Buggs who did it. 'I mean, this town can be so *small-minded*.'

My brain jumps, like *it's a sign, dummy!* Our love, I think. Sasha and me. The town would never accept us. We'd have to run away. I grin like an idiot.

'What are you smiling at?' Sasha raises an eyebrow like she's been tricked. The sliding door opens behind us and Sasha swings around in her chair to see who it is.

'Nothing,' I say. 'Just...thanks. This is nice.' On the word *nice* my voice breaks, just a little.

Sasha turns back around, waves her hand like *whatever, don't mention it*. She says, 'Do you think he's going to jail?'

'My dad? I don't know.'

'It must be horrible, not knowing.' She fixes me with this really beautiful stare and suddenly I want us to be old together, talking on a porch with all this history between us, all our edges worn down, all our thoughts already known, so it's just *safe*.

'It's hard,' I say. 'He used to be so fun. He used to have this crazy beard that was ginger even though his hair was brown and he'd always be laughing. Then he hurt his back and he couldn't work.'

Sasha nods.

'He worked for the council. Helped with the land-scaping. All that stuff on the main street especially. One day he's lifting a bag of fertiliser and his back just goes. Council gave him bugger all compo.'

'My uncle's on compo but he still works. He's like those guys they catch on *A Current Affair* and that.'

'Dad couldn't hardly move for, like, two months. The money didn't even cover the medical bills, and Mum had to get extra work. Then, cause he hasn't got much educa-tion, cause he's got a record, the only job he's good for is traffic duty. Holding up a stop-and-go sign.'

Sasha stops spinning her milkshake. 'You're dad's got a record? What for?'

'Um.' I'm suddenly super-thirsty, even though I'm half-full of caramel milk. I realise I've just told Sasha more about my family in five minutes than I've told anyone in sixteen years.

'It was ages ago,' I say. 'He was only twenty-some-thing. Got done for speeding and the cop went on with it and you know...'

'He fought a cop?'

'I don't really...I don't know the details.' Jesus. Why couldn't I just say *no*?

'That's so cool. My dad just fucked off when Mum told him she was pregnant. Apparently.'

'Shit.'

'It is what it is. Who needs men, anyway?' She has a

weird smirk on her face, and I laugh like it's really funny.

'Not us!' I say. Disney princess. I remind myself to die from embarrassment later.

'Will your mum have to go back to work now?' says Sasha. 'What does she do?'

'Supply teacher. She works already, but, yeah, she'll have to pick up some extra work.'

'What about your brother?'

'Angus?'

'Yeah, Angus.'

'What about him?'

'What does he do?'

I make a *peh* noise. 'As little as possible.'

'Didn't he go to uni?'

'For a little while. He didn't last though.'

'Why not?'

'Cause he's a lazy tool.'

Sasha laughs, her nose crinkling up. 'That's funny.'

I laugh as well. 'He's got this new plan now,' I say. Making fun of my brother seems like safer ground. 'He's trying to catch the Beast of Barwen.'

'The what?'

'It's this creature that's supposed to live up in the mountains outside of town. Every couple of years someone says they've seen it.'

'Oh, right. Like the big cat or whatever?'

'Yeah. It's in the paper every once in a while. He's got all this equipment, like a video camera, and he's set it up all in this hideout, like, with sticks covering it and stuff. It's ridiculous.'

I wait for Sasha to laugh again but instead she goes all serious and says, 'I want to see it.'

'The hideout?'

'Yes. It sounds amazing.'

'It's really stupid. It's like what a five-year-old kid would do.'

'It sounds *amazing*.' She takes my hand across the table and squeezes my fingers. 'Promise you'll take me there.'

'Well I don't know if—'

'Take me there *right now*, Clancy.' She's looking me right in the eyes and I notice a thin trail of blonde hairs running along the top of her left eyebrow.

'I don't really know the way.'

'We'll get Angus, then. We'll all go together. It sounds so crazy. *The Beast of Barwen*.' She says it really low and growly and I know she's making fun of it but it means I'll do anything not to let her leave. 'Gimme your phone,' she says. 'I'll call Angus.'

'I don't have...I don't have it on me.' My ears burn hot.

'Let's go and get him then. It'll be an adventure!' Sasha slurps up the last of her milkshake, tipping the container up to get the dregs.

Most of me is saying *NO*. Most of me knows this is the sort of thing I never do. Most of me is built entirely out of denial and indecision and safety. But she's *right here*, the literal girl of my dreams. There's a hollow at the base of her neck, so soft that my finger could rest there and I'd hardly feel it. A part of her made just for me.

'Sure,' I say. 'An adventure. Why not?'

We're cruising back towards my house. This is fine, I tell myself. This is cool. And, in fact there *is* something cool about driving up these familiar streets in the front seat of a different car. My stomach's churning with milk and sugar and nicotine but this is kind of exciting. I keep stealing glances at Sasha's legs. She's so incredibly cool, and she's not even trying. That's what makes it cool, I guess. She isn't a tryhard like Nancy, with her fancy clothes, with her pretend niceness. I sort of feel bad about what I said to Nancy, but I don't want to think about that now.

We round the top of the driveway with music blaring, and I hope to hell Mum's not back from work yet. Her car's not there but Angus is sitting on the verandah, his shirt off, with a beer in one hand and, for some reason, a tennis racquet in the other. He gets up when he sees the car, lifts up his aviators. It takes me a moment before I realise he probably thinks it's Buggs.

'Drive down if you like,' I say to Sasha, with the casual air of someone who always does whatever they like. Sasha shunts down a gear and roars towards the front door. It's pretty funny to watch Angus try and prepare himself for what he thinks is going to be a confrontation. I want my first car to have tinted windows.

We stop and I wave an arm out the window at him. 'Hey Spangus!' I shout. Sasha laughs and my confidence triples. I get out of the car, enjoying the confusion on my brother's face. I go, 'What's shaking, dickweed?' and he just looks at me like *what the hell?* Sasha gets out of the drivers side.

'What's going on?' Angus says to me.

'Thought we'd pay you a little visit,' I say.

'Hey, Angus,' says Sasha.

'Hey,' he says. 'What's happening?'

'We want to go on an adventure with you!' she says, hooking her thumbs into her belt loops.

'What?'

'We want to catch the beast with you,' I say.

'Sorry?' Angus moves his jaw like he's got gum in his mouth, but he hasn't.

'The Beast of Barwen,' says Sasha. 'I heard all about it. I want to help. *We* want to help.'

Sasha puts her arm around me and the feeling of her weight against me makes me shiver. She's strong and soft and the word *womanly* enters my head, which is pretty weird. My bony shoulder will probably leave her a bruise.

'I don't know what you're talking about,' says Angus. He taps the tennis racquet against his leg.

'I think it sounds *so* interesting,' says Sasha. 'You must have done a heap of research.'

'Yeah, well, it's not something you can fast-track.' He puffs out his chest. Boys are so predictable.

'I'd love to have a look at the set-up,' she says. 'It sounds so *adventurous*.

'I suppose so,' Angus says. 'But I've already been up there today, and I've already had a few of these.' He waggles the beer at us. 'And I'd like to have a few more. Plus I'm babysitting.'

I go, 'Who left *you* in charge?' and I know I'm being a dick, but only because Sasha Strickland has her arm around me.

'You weren't anywhere to be seen,' says Angus. 'Anyway, I'm a great babysitter. Watch this.' He puts down the beer and cups his hand around his mouth. 'TITCH! HEY, TITCH!'

Footsteps, and then Titch comes running round the side of the verandah, his little square face red from effort. He's got a plastic army man in his hand. 'Hey, Pants,' he says to me. I shoot eye daggers at him. 'Is that your *giiiiirlfriend*?' he says. I splutter out a complete lack of response and Angus laughs.

'Is that your *booooyfriend*?' says Sasha, pointing to the army man.

'No!' says Titch, holding it up to show her. 'He's got

fourteen grenades and they'd be like, *pkhooew!*' He mimes a massive explosion. If there was a career that rewarded the ability to recreate the sounds of military damage, Titch would be set for life.

'Ready to go, soldier?' Angus brandishes the tennis racquet.

Titch drops the army man. 'Yeah!'

'All right.' Angus comes down the front steps and picks up a tennis ball that's lying with a bunch of others in the grass. He turns around, throws the ball up and whacks it from underneath with the racquet. The ball flies up high above the roof and I see it hit the other side and bounce up again. Titch sprints around the side of the house going, 'Got it got it got it!'

Angus turns back to us and gives a little bow. 'And that,' he says, 'is how you babysit.'

'Impressive,' says Sasha.

'We call it House Bounce,' he says. 'You never know which way it's going to bounce. If you catch it on the full, the other person has to chase it.'

'Doesn't it get caught in the gutters?' says Sasha.

'Not our gutters. They're clogged as hell.'

'You were supposed to clean them months ago,' I say.

'What's the point?' says Angus. He swings the racquet a few times, trying to look professional, trying to show off his pathetic muscles.

I stare past him at the pink outline of the graffiti. 'So can we go up to the hideout?'

'Not today,' he says. 'Tomorrow maybe, if you're good.'

'Can't tomorrow,' says Sasha. 'Working. Day after's Saturday, though.'

'Have to be the arvo,' says Angus. 'I got some stuff to do in the morning.'

I make a wanking motion with my hand, which he pretends to ignore.

'Okay,' says Sasha. 'Saturday arvo. Want to meet in town? Round three?'

'Probably just leave from here,' says Angus.

'Outside the library,' says Sasha, ignoring him. 'There's always parks there. Catch you then.' She takes her arm from around me and I nearly fall over because I've been leaning into her so much.

'Bye,' I say.

She does a little wave, hops back in the car, and reverses up the driveway.

When she's gone, Angus bursts out laughing. 'Sasha *Strickland*,' he says. 'What the actual fuck?'

'We're just hanging out,' I say, as coolly as I can. I know I'm going to cop a heap of shit, but I don't care. Today is one of the all-time great days. And I get to see her again.

'I can't believe you told her about the hideout.'

'It's not a secret.'

'Not now it's not.'

'You could've said no.'

'It's okay,' he says. 'We'll just blindfold her. I'm sure you'd like to do the honours.'

'What's that supposed to mean?'

Angus slowly raises two fingers to his mouth in a V shape and waggles his tongue between them.

I pick up another tennis ball from the grass and House Bounce it straight into his nuts.

*I'm in such* a good mood that I get Titch to help me make burgers, forming our own patties from some mince I found in the freezer. Titch shapes them up after I make sure he's washed his hands at least twice. I make the salad and even cook onions so when Mum comes in the door after work looking like she's been through a war, there's dinner waiting.

Titch and Angus and I have already eaten ours watching *The Simpsons* but when I ask Mum what she wants on her burger she just says, 'I'm not really hungry, Clancy,' and then, 'Am I supposed to clean all this up?' and I give her a look like *for God's sake, I tried*, and she just stares back at me, so I give her another face like *it's not like you were here to cook us dinner*.

She hangs her bag up and goes to me, 'Do you know a girl called Nancy DeRosa?'

Shit.

I go, 'Who?' as if this will end the conversation.

'I don't have time for this, Clancy. I've been talking to her mother for the last half an hour.'

I start to sweat a little. I should have had a shower. I'd be dead if she knew I'd been smoking.

'Her mother,' Mum rubs her forehead with the palm of her hand, 'is Carla DeRosa. New vice principal at St Stephen's. I'm about to finish for the day and start the *three quarter of an hour* drive home when I get this call out of nowhere.' Mum takes her mobile out of her bag and unclips the battery. 'This is just for you guys to call. God knows how she got the number.'

The burger in my stomach starts complaining. George Parry had our emergency contacts, and mine was Mum's mobile.

'Apparently you *abused* her daughter at Nature Club!' Mum throws up her hands.

'I didn't abuse her. That makes it sound like I'm a priest.'

'Now is *not* the time for jokes, Clancy. You do know this girl, then? You did talk to her today?'

'Yes. But she was being really...' I couldn't even come up with a good lie.

'You *swore* at her, her mother says.'

I realise I've got no way out of this. 'It wasn't even like that.'

'What was it like, then?'

'Doesn't matter,' I say. 'You wouldn't even understand. You wouldn't even want to.'

'That's great,' says Mum. 'And now you won't tell me anything. As usual.'

My legs are shaking. I keep my mouth shut. I'm not going to play the game.

Mum's face falls. 'Impossible,' she says. 'It's impossible. Why am I the only person who feels like they have to take responsibility in this family? You didn't even tell us you were going. What if something happened to you?'

'Who was I supposed to tell, Mum? You were out, Angus was out, Dad was...It doesn't work like that. I needed to get out of the house.'

Mum sits down at the kitchen table. 'Can't even keep one surface clean.' She picks up a handful of paper—old homework, magazines, unanswered mail—and holds it up in the air. Then she just stares at it, as if it's going to talk.

'You'll have to apologise,' she says eventually.

'For what?'

'For whatever you said to that Nancy girl. You refuse to talk about it, so I'm just going to assume the worst.' Mum puts down the handful of paper. 'You're going over there to apologise.'

'Going over where?'

'To the DeRosas'.'

'To their house?'

'Yes, Clancy. To their house. Tomorrow. Her mother insisted.' Mum rubs her eyes. 'As if I don't have enough to do already.'

I stand there, shaking my head. 'This is so unfair.'

'Why is it unfair, Clancy? Tell me why.'

I can't, of course, because that would mean telling her about Raylene McCarthy and Buggs and all the shit I have to put up with on an everyday basis. Mum doesn't need to know all that on top of everything else. As good as it would feel to wound her, as satisfying as it would be to let her know I'm going through a heap of shit as well, she doesn't deserve it. And I don't deserve the inevitable follow-up, the heart-to-hearts and worried looks.

Besides, I'm not a squealer like Nancy. Nancy's mum—Carla, what a ridiculous name—would've probably taken Nancy out straight away to buy new clothes or get her hair done or some other bullshit. Anything to keep the spoiled little brat happy.

'I'm tired,' I say.

The word *tired* seems to hit Mum like an arrow. She slumps back in the chair. 'Let's just get it over and done with,' she says. 'And then obviously you won't do *anything* like this again.'

'Fine.'

'I'm having a shower,' says Mum, her parenting done for the day. I know I won't see her now until the morning. I rinse off my dinner plate and leave the rest for Angus, who agreed to wash up but I know won't do it.

I've already decided that when Sasha and I live together, we won't eat until nine at night, like in the movies. We'll eat olives and bread and ham so there won't be any cooking and only a few plates to clean up. We'll live somewhere by the water, but where the nights are cool, so we won't have to fight for who gets to sit next to the fan and our legs won't stick to the couch. We'll have wine and talk until the sun comes up. It'll be so far from here that we'll both forget where we even came from. There'll be no apologies, no responsibility, no family.

As predicted, when I come back to the lounge room, Titch and Angus have both disappeared. I watch TV for a bit but I'm not really taking it in so I got back into the kitchen and take the last two patties out of the fridge and cook up a double with cheese. I wrap it up in greaseproof paper and take it out the back. The light's on in the shed and I smile. I knock on the garage door and shout, 'I have your dinner Meester Underhill!' like some fancy waiter. Dad rolls up the door and he's sort of smiling, like *how weird is my daughter, anyway?* but I don't care. I lift up the top piece of bread on his burger and make it go, 'Where would you like me? In your mouth?'

Dad laughs, shaking his head. 'Talking burger,' he says. 'This is a treat. You make this?'

'Sure did.'

Thumb over the shoulder. 'Come on, then.'

There's paper all over the workbench and a bottle of Bundy instead of beer. 'What's all this?' I say.

'Just some paperwork.'

'For what?'

'Just stuff I have to get done.'

I sit down in the bucket seat and it rocks crazily.

'There's still an ice-cream left,' Dad says.

I lean over and open the esky. The Cornetto's floating in lukewarm water and when I press it with my fingers it's squidgy. 'Thanks for that, Dad.'

He laughs. 'Good burger, though.'

'Maybe I can have some of that rum then,' I say. 'Seeing as you've failed to look after my ice-cream.'

'No way, kiddo, you know what this stuff costs? Don't want to waste it on an underdeveloped palate.'

'What's the score in the cricket?'

'Hasn't started yet. We're eighty in front but only got three wickets left. Pitch's turning square apparently.'

'I'd like to listen to some when it starts.' I want to spend as long as I can here. The shed, with Dad, is international waters for real emotions.

'Hey,' says Dad, 'what do you want for your birthday?'

'My birthday? That's not till December.'

Dad talks through a mouthful of burger: 'I'm getting organised this year.'

'I'd like driving lessons,' I say. 'Starting next week.'

'Nope.'

'Come on! I *know* I'll be a good driver.'

'Not till you're seventeen.'

'Aagh!'

'You know the rule.'

'The rule's *ridiculous*. You haven't even *seen* me drive. I might be amazing.'

'It doesn't matter. It's the law.'

'I'm still allowed to practise.'

'Too many people drive too soon, Clancy. I don't want you to get into—' Dad stops himself. 'I don't want you getting into trouble. I want you to be safe.'

Shit. Our driving argument has been going for years, but I had to bring it up tonight. 'Sorry,' I say. 'I didn't...'

'It's fine,' he says. 'Don't worry about it.'

Now I feel terrible. I say, 'I should get back inside.'

'You don't have to,' Dad says. 'It's nothing to do with you.'

'I just feel bad.'

Dad fills up his glass. 'Thanks for the burger. Did you make them for everyone?'

'Yeah.'

'I'm sure your mum appreciates it. It hasn't been easy for her, last couple of days.'

'Maybe,' I say. 'She got back ages late.' I decide not to tell him the stuff about Nancy and her mum. He'll find out later, anyway, and why ruin a perfectly nice evening?

'It's tough. We're trying to work it out.' He leans back in his chair and stares at the ceiling. We can hear the whine of mosquitoes outside the windows.

A sudden sadness wells up at the thought that Dad

might not be able to sit in his shed again. 'Will you have to go to prison?' I say. 'I know you didn't do anything, but…'

Dad rubs his eyes. 'There's still an investigation,' he says. 'They've told me not to leave town, but no one's talking about prison.'

'Okay.'

'I know it's tough on you kids, too, but we've just got to wait it out.'

'What about your job?'

'That's something for down the track as well. For now we just have to wait and see.'

I glance up at the papers on bench. 'Are you doing, like, legal stuff? Is that what the papers are?'

He looks down at them. 'Just sorting a few things out. You know me. Prepared as ever.'

'You know you don't have to get me a birthday present this year, or a Christmas present or anything if it'll make it easier.'

Dad puts his hand up to his mouth. 'Aw Jeez.' He shakes his head. 'You're a good kid, Clance.' His face crumples and he's suddenly a stranger. My dad doesn't do this. I get up to put my hand on his arm and he gathers me in and hugs me like he hasn't done since I was little and I smell the rum and his arms are so strong and then I'm crying too. I push my face into his T-shirt and I never want him to be anywhere else ever again.

*The whole night* I don't even bother turning off the light; I know I'm not getting to sleep. When my head's like this, all I can do is stare at a corner of the ceiling. Staring for Australia. Gold medal in the eight-hour Mind Race. The worst thing is, I've never been able to focus on just one problem at a time. Tonight is no different. Nancy, Sasha, Dad. Over and over. I lie there, still in my clothes, paralysed by the logjam of my thoughts.

I know—I'm smart enough to know—this is textbook teenage angst, but it doesn't make it any easier. A whole bunch of useless TV drama tears make the pillow wet so I can't turn my head. I clench and unclench my fists and I'm not sure who or what I really feel sorry for.

*Make a list*, the tiny rational part of me says, the part of me who checks psychology books out of the library, knowing full well that the only people who check psychology books out of the library are people who think they're too good for self-help books. People who know they've got problems but are too proud to admit it.

And the question at the base of it all, as always, is: what am I doing? Just a simple question: what am I all about?

The Sasha stuff.

I can cut it any way I want but I can't get away from what it means. I am obsessed. I am paralysed. I am in love. I am whatever it is when you're my age and you're adrift and all your hormones are holding a cold gun to your head. But it's all about a *girl*. Is this a minor detail? Does it even matter?

My whole life, pretty much, has been back to front. When I was little, I knew I was supposed to wear dresses and dream of princesses and run away shrieking from boys in the playground, but I never wanted to. I remember being far more interested in the things I wasn't supposed to be interested in. I don't think that has really changed.

Past the age of maybe eight, I've never really *got* boys. My brothers are presumably a poor sample set, but if that's the case, so are all the other boys I've known. And now I'm at an age where my life is supposed to revolve around them. I'm supposed to start wearing tight dresses and drinking pre-mixed spirits and generally generating all my self-worth from some guy's attention. And it's not that I hate guys, but they're just...in the shadow cast by the larger part of me. The part that's interested in girls.

This is the word I always use with myself. *Interested*. As if that stuff—gender orientation, whatever—is something to be coolly appreciated. As if I'm casting an eye over an interesting building or I'm walking, detached but aware, through an art gallery. I can't even tell myself who I am.

I roll over and there's Dolly Parton's life lying half-open on the bed. Dolly wouldn't care who I loved or what I obsessed about. In music, pain is money. Maybe I should buy a guitar and start a new career. Where else could so much emotional crap make you so successful? Except no one would care about the turmoil of a weird, ambiguous white girl. White-ish.

Then I think, would Dad be allowed to play music in jail? Could he have books? Could he listen to the cricket on the radio?

These are the things I would be afraid of if I went to prison:

1) Forced exercise
2) Sharing a toilet with other people
3) Having to eat meals with other people
4) Any type of forced therapy
5) Having to say hello to your cellmate every day.

The sex crimes and the stabbings and the drugs up your arse and the neo-nazi groups? Neither here nor there. The real hell would be having no time to yourself.

I scrunch up my eyes, trying to stop my thoughts. My brain deals with real shit, always, by turning it into a joke, some kind of psychological stand-up routine. But this isn't funny. Dad is really in trouble. I think about all the paperwork in the shed, about him trying to sort everything out.

If he went to jail, everything would go to shit. I don't even want to imagine it. Mum would have to get full-time work. I'd have to look after the house. Angus would have to get a job. Titch would have to do *something*. We'd visit Dad on the weekends, talk through glass.

A noise escapes my mouth, a deep moan, and it shocks me so much that I clamp my hand over my mouth. But it comes again, and I'm moaning like a cartoon ghost and I can't stop and it's like something inside me has uncorked and all this deep, horrible sadness is pouring out of me.

I clamp a pillow over my face and I hear myself saying over and over *stop crying you stupid fucking faggy bogan chickenshit you can't do anything right and nobody likes you and nothing will ever ever ever change.* I hold the pillow down harder until I can smell my own sweat and Mum's geranium detergent and the fabric opens and shuts over my nostrils. I'm trying to smother myself but of course I can't make it actually happen. Like trying to hold your breath underwater until you drown.

I take the pillow off and lie there for a few amazing moments where my brain has actually turned itself off and all that I feel is my heart hammering, my breath catching back up to itself. There's something scary but exhilarating about it. A momentary loss of control. Then my mind starts up again but I focus intently on the corner of my wardrobe and make myself think about how the pieces of wood all fit together and who decided that a square was going to be a square and how did we come so far from just a couple of hairy people and some rocks and now we've got computers and who was in charge of thinking up these things and how did someone know how to make anything and was it just hard work or did you have to be born a genius and then my thoughts settle down to a gentle hum and I close my eyes and I'm suddenly as tired as I've ever been.

Another death, I think, another day. Tomorrow we'll all try again.

We're in the car by 10 am, and Mum's still dirty with me. I remain as calm as possible. This, I tell myself, is the least of my worries. This morning is a drop in the shitty ocean that is my life. I ignore Mum's constant stink-eye, and don't say a thing when she puts the radio on Classic Hits and cranks it up. As Elton John craps on about some bland collection of emotions, I stay as silent as I can. Mum's drumming her fingers on the steering wheel, trying her best to get me to tell her to stop, but I've been around too long to fall for that old trick. I pull up my hoodie—she hates that—and sink as low as I can into the seat.

It's only as we're driving through town that I start to wonder where Nancy actually lives. I'd assumed she'd be in a brand new house, one of those estates where the streets are named after wines and native flowers. But instead we're heading out of town, turning right on the so-called Tourist Trail, named this because it leads away from Barwen and on to towns that people might want to visit. I want to ask Mum where we're going, but that would require me speaking to her.

Soon, the car slows down and I can see Mum scanning either side of the road, her head rotating slowly like a side-show clown. Then she stops the car and says, suddenly, 'Oh.'

We're right outside a motel, according to the sign. Actually the *Westside Motel*, one of the long, nondescript brick accommodations that line the road out of town. A big Foxtel logo and an unlit neon sign saying *Danny's Ristorant* are both attached to the reception building.

'They live in a motel?' I say.

Mum goes, 'I guess so.' She takes a scrap of paper from her pocket and examines it, like maybe she's written the number upside down. 'I guess so.'

Then we see Carla waiting by the entrance, wearing one of those puffy mountaineering jackets, even though it's not very cold. She give us a quick wave, and Mum drives through into the carpark.

'Good morning,' says Carla when we get out of the car. She doesn't seem angry with me, but she also doesn't seem particularly happy to see us. 'It's the best they could do for now,' she says, gesturing around her. 'There was supposed to be temporary accommodation at St Stephen's, but,' she waves her hands, 'budgets, cutbacks, shortages. The usual stuff.'

'Doesn't surprise me,' says Mum, in a weird, light voice. 'I know the world well.' She seems to have been blindsided by the location. I was sure she was going to be in teacher-voice mode all day.

'Hello, Clancy,' Carla says. 'Nancy is inside. We'll be just on the other side.' She points to a brown door—one in a line of many—that's slightly ajar.

'Oh,' I say. 'Okay.' I walk over to it, waiting for a moment to see if the two mums are going to follow me, but they're not moving. All right, I say to myself. This is one of those *you've got yourself into this mess, you get yourself out of it* kind of situations.

I push open the door, and the sanitised smell of commercial cleaner hits me. It's exactly what you'd expect a motel room on the outskirts of a shithole country town to look like. A double and single bed, two Steve Parish photos framed on the walls, everything washed in weak, lace-curtained light. How long have they had to live here? A large suitcase is open against the opposite wall. Nancy's sitting at the end of the double bed, in tracksuit pants and a woollen jumper.

'So, hi,' I say, realising I haven't actually prepared myself for this. 'This is, um…they're nice photos.'

Nancy lifts her head to take in the framed view of Uluru she's probably only stared at a thousand times already. 'Hi,' she says. Her hands are twisted up in the ends of her jumper. I can't read her. She's not hostile, but maybe just unsure, like she hasn't yet decided how to react to me.

'So listen, about the other day…' This seems as good

a place as any to start. I feel sick, stomach sick. 'I really was a massive dick.'

'No, it's okay.' Her voice is hardly audible. A fan rattles from what I imagine is the bathroom around the corner.

'No,' I say, and I realise this is actually what I think. 'It's not okay. I shouldn't have had a go at you. You were just trying to be nice.'

Nancy rubs her eyes and I see she's crying. 'It's me,' she says. 'I never pick the right moments. I shouldn't even have said anything to Mum.'

I feel the glare of both mothers on the back of my neck so I step inside and close the door. 'No, you really should have. I was a real jerk. I want to apologise.'

'I should be apologising.' Nancy rubs her eyes with her sleeve.

I go, 'We're quite bad at this, aren't we?' and Nancy nods. I sit down on the end of the single bed. 'Look,' I say, 'I'm really sorry. Please accept my apology, sincerely, even if only for the two mums waiting outside in a motel carpark, thinking they're parenting.'

Nancy smiles. 'They'll be in the next room.' She drums the wall behind her with her fingers. 'They're joined. This is my wing of the mansion.'

'Oh, right. Could we break a vase, just to give them something to think about? Would you have to pay for it?'

'No, I think St Stephen's could come up with the twelve bucks.'

I laugh. 'How long do you have to stay here for?' I go

to bounce on the bed, but it's so soft I just sink into it. 'Jesus.'

'I know. It's like sleeping in a marshmallow.' She falls back on the double bed. 'This one is just as bad. Feel it.'

I get up and flop down next to her. Something deep in the frame creaks worryingly. 'Man,' I say. 'Authentic country charm.'

'We were only supposed to be here for a few nights, but it's already been two weeks.'

'I feel like your human rights are being impinged upon. And I say that without really knowing what *impinged* means.'

'Next week, apparently. They've got a place for us. A real house.'

'Bet you're counting down the days.' I turn over so we're both on our backs. 'Oh, I'd hoped there would be a mirror on the ceiling.'

'Can't even get *that* right.'

We lie there for a while and I hear a clock ticking. I turn my head to face her. 'I really am sorry,' I say.

'Shut up about it, then.' Nancy grins.

I sit up. 'Should we let our mothers in? Tell them we're BFFs forever?'

'Nah,' Nancy says. 'I need every moment away from that woman I can get. She's fine, but...you know.'

'I do know.'

Nancy yawns. 'It's not easy for her, the move, but at least she's got work to keep her occupied. I'm just here. We haven't even got all our stuff yet. They can't send it down until we have somewhere to send it. I've got a couple of suitcases, and that's about it.'

I feel extra bad for Nancy, then. At least I have my own room, my own refuge from all the crap that goes on outside your bedroom door. 'So will you get to go back to Brisbane in the meantime? Or call your friends or whatever?'

Nancy sort of grimaces. 'Not really an option.'

'Oh. Why's that?'

'There's sort of…complications there.'

'In Brisbane?'

'At my old school. There was some stuff. Some crap. That happened.' Nancy's voice sounds like she's reciting a poem from memory. 'Bullying. Was what it was.'

'Shit. Sorry.'

Nancy shrugs. 'It happens. It happened.' She smiles at me, a really unconvincing smile. 'Private school. All girls. Actual hell on earth.'

I try to think of a joke to lighten the mood, but nothing really fits. I give her time instead.

Nancy's mouth is the sketch of a straight line. She says, 'I'm the reason we're here. We moved because of me, because I couldn't hack it. Mum's uprooted her life and her job and…everything, all because of me.' She starts to cry, and I take her hand and squeeze it. Her cheeks are shining. 'I can't complain. I can't *ever* complain. Because it's my fault.'

I go, 'Don't say that.' That's how people on TV respond at times like this.

'I've got this *procedure*,' she says, finger-quoting. 'I have to go through it whenever I feel threatened. I have to tell Mum. That's part of our *emotional contract*. That's why I told her about you. I had to. It's so stupid.'

'No, it's not.'

'Well, anyway, it's part of this manual this psychologist gave Mum. Like I'm a car and he's a mechanic.'

'Charming.'

'Yeah. I mean, it's fine I guess. It sort of works. I still have to see a counsellor. Except now we have to do it over Skype. So modern.' She laughs again, humourlessly.

'e-Shrink,' I say, without thinking.

'Exactly.'

'Jesus. All that bullshit I said to you.'

'I've heard worse.' She laughs, humourlessly.

'What did...did someone hurt you, or...' I feel like a creep. 'Don't answer that. You don't have to—'

'Not, like *sticks and stones*. I just wasn't into all the social bullshit. All the groups and cliques. The clichéd shit. I just became the go-to girl. Whenever people felt angry or frustrated or wanted to let off some steam, they knew they could take it out on me. And yeah, not just calling names. Sly, horrible shit.'

'God. That's awful.'

'That's the real version anyway. Clinically speaking I was *the vessel for other people's unhappiness with their own lives.* Which is a great and clever thing to say to someone who's being...tormented. *It's their problem, not yours.*'

'Jeez.'

'It might be their problem, but I was the one who couldn't leave the house or even go *online*. This counsellor is useless. He thinks I'm a logic puzzle or something. It's like he can't see me as a human.'

'That's awful.' I want so badly to tell her about Raylene McCarthy and Buggs and how I feel every time someone shouts *faggot* from a passing car. I want her to know some of us know what she's going through. Except I don't know how.

Then Nancy goes, 'Let's actually be friends. You and me.' Her expression opens up and I see the Nancy who greets me happily every time at Nature Club. She is hopelessly innocent, I realise. She is a relentless optimist in a world that crushes earnestness and trust into small cubes of fear.

'I know it's like something you say in grade three,' she says, 'but let's actually be friends.'

'I'm in,' I say, without a second's hesitation.

'Awesome!' Her face drops for a moment. 'Let's just make an agreement,' she says, 'to not have any other bullshit. Let's just say *let's be friends* and tell each other stuff and hang out because I think you're very cool and I think I'm very cool and so that should work out well, right?'

It's a rare type of thrill I'm feeling now. A calming,

soothing thing. Maybe it's happiness. 'I don't have a phone,' I say.

'So?'

'I'm just getting all the bad things about me out of the way.'

'Okay. Well, I'm emotionally damaged, obviously.'

'I'm emotionally stunted.'

'I have to write letters to my own feelings. Every week.'

'I hang out at a skate park, and I don't even like skating.'

'I spend all my time with my mother.'

'My family don't talk to each other.'

'My dad lives in another country.'

'My dad—' And I stop. I can feel my body physically rejecting emotional openness. I can work up to it. 'The whole town thinks my dad's done something horrible. They...think my entire family are criminals.'

Nancy hardly even reacts. 'I have to eat cereal out of one of those little mini boxes every morning.'

'Like, a travel pack?'

She nods.

'Do you at least get Coco Pops?'

'It's only ever Special K or cornflakes.'

'That's some stone cold shit.'

She laughs.

I smile too. It's fine, I think, that I'm not telling her my one, actual secret. It's fine.

*And then suddenly* it's mums and daughters at twenty paces. And by this I mean side-by-side in a booth in *Danny's Ristorant*, which I can safely say is the saddest place I have ever been. Even though the sun's blazing outside, even though it's a bright shiny spring day, inside the cafe it's drab and dark green and I get the feeling everything in this place once got very wet and has never had a chance to dry.

Mum's sitting next to me and her voice is light and fluffy and she's laughing and acting like a normal person and I can't make fun of her because we're in company. She and Carla, it seems, have been bonding over teaching stories in the other room while Nancy and I talked. Everyone has made friends and it is really, really, weird.

The owner of the cafe, who is possibly the Patient Zero of the rising damp smell, serves us what he no doubt considers coffee.

'Thanks, Danny,' says Carla.

'Great customers, these two,' says Danny. 'Wish there were more like them.'

Nancy gives me wide eyes across the table.

'Are you joining us here as well?' he says to Mum.

'No,' she says, 'but it's a lovely place you've made here.'

I snort a laugh and quickly turn it into a cough. Nancy keeps her face stony solid, but raises a single eyebrow. I have to look away.

'I'll be sorry to see you both go,' Danny says. 'Usually only get people here for a night or two. Always passing through.' He wipes his hands on the front of the apron he's wearing. 'You need anything else, you give me a yell.'

'Shall do,' says Carla. 'Thanks.'

When he's safely beyond earshot, I'm forced into another coughing fit and Nancy kicks my foot. Our mothers remain oblivious.

'This is lovely,' says Mum, for the fortieth time. I guess it's a rarity for her as well, having someone to talk to.

'It'll be nice when we get our own place, though. Won't it, sweetie?' Carla puts her arm around Nancy. 'Be a bit more like home.'

'Yeah,' says Nancy. 'Definitely.'

'Not that this place is *too* bad,' says Carla, looking at me for some reason. 'It's nice Danny gave us the adjoining rooms.'

'Oh man,' Nancy says to me. 'There's this portrait opposite Mum's bed. I swear Danny's cut out the eyeholes.'

'Nancy. Please.' Carla has her own teacher voice, which is kind of chilling.

Nancy lowers her voice. 'One time, with breakfast, there was this rose in a vase.'

'His mother grows roses,' says Carla, ignoring her. 'It was very pretty.'

'Country hospitality,' Mum says. 'Lovely.'

'I miss my mirror, mainly,' Carla says. 'There's no full-length here, just the little one in the bathroom.' She stirs a sweetener into her coffee. 'A girl gets to know her mirror, you know? You trust it, after a while. Or at least you know the best way to look good in it.'

Mum giggles, and the need to escape rises in me like bile. We're sailing dangerously close to a moment where Mum suggests we all form a bookclub. She once used the phrase *Stitch 'n' Bitch* in my presence, and I made it quickly and violently clear she never should again.

'I could never give up my mirror,' Mum says.

I say, 'A full-length mirror is literally my worst enemy. I spend so much of my day trying to forget what I look like. Why do I need something whose job it is to remind me?'

'Agreed,' says Nancy.

Mum looks at me with a mixture of confusion and, strangely, admiration. Like *my daughter is still strange, but is she at the same time contributing to a conversation?*

'You're beautiful, Clancy,' says Carla. 'Now where did your name come from, anyway? I love it.'

'I am a product of an inexplicable love of bush poetry,' I say, which is the line I always use.

'*Clancy of the Overflow*,' says Mum. 'Bob's favourite poem. I think it's kind of sweet.'

'And yet he failed to name either *boy* in our family the boy's name.'

'It fits you though, darling.'

'Wow. Thanks.'

Nancy goes, 'I got my name cause Mum liked Nancy Sinatra.'

'Hmm,' I say. 'Only two letters different, and suddenly it's a normal name.' I give Mum a glare, but she continues to be immune to embarrassment. Her and Carla share a look. *Our daughters are so individual and amazing and aren't we blessed their screwed-up lives make ours look more normal?*

Mum takes a look at her watch. 'This is so lovely, but we've really got to go. I've got to get to work.'

'Thanks for coming out here,' says Carla. 'It wasn't under the best circumstances, but I think it's turned out well.'

'I do hope we'll do it again,' says Mum. Then she raises her index finger, as if struck by divine inspiration. 'Sunday!' she says. 'Come over for lunch. Sunday lunch is something of a tradition in the Underhill household.'

This is news to me.

'If we're not imposing,' says Carla.

'Not at all. The more the merrier.'

Good luck to you, lady, I think. Try getting our family to be in one place for more than five minutes. *Something of a tradition*, indeed.

'Lovely,' says Carla.

'Lovely,' says Mum.

Nancy and just look at each other, like *yep*.

*Carla and Mum* talk by the car, tapping each other's number into their phones. I don't think I've ever seen my mother so excited.

Nancy and I say goodbye, and we even go to hug, which is awkward because we're leaning towards each other like a bridge, trying to keep our bodies apart. We laugh at this, knowing it means we're really alike. Just two modern ladies bonding over debilitating intimacy and trust issues.

'Can I text you later?' she says.

'No phone, remember?'

'Really?'

'I wasn't joking.'

'This must be what it's like to be friends with a Mormon.'

'You won't be complaining when I churn us up some fresh butter.'

'You got email? I'm not allowed on Facebook or

anything. Not that I'd want it again.'

'Right. Yeah. I've got an email account, but I usually check it at school. We've only got one computer at home, in the kitchen. So...'

Nancy laughs. 'So, do I just send up a signal into the sky when I want to contact you?'

'Yes. Only at night, when there's a bit of cloud around. I'll email you this arvo, though. Promise.' A mobile phone starts to overtake new shoes in my imaginary budget.

'Cool. Well I guess I'll see you on Sunday, anyway.'

'For sure.'

'Okay.'

And then we're attempting another awkward goodbye. I think maybe I should kiss her cheek but then she sort of bows so I end up kissing the top of her head. We pull apart, and the secret look of the terminally awkward passes between us: *Let us never speak of this mortifying moment again, upon pain of death.*

Mum appears next to me and says, 'Come on, kiddo,' like this is the sort of relationship we have.

'Okay.' I need to get away before I do anything else embarrassing. A curious mix of shame and elation fills me as I get into the car, and we drive away, waving.

'That went very well, I thought,' says Mum.

'Have you always called me *kiddo* and I've only now just noticed?'

She ignores this. 'So you've made up with Nancy, obviously.'

163

'Yeah.'

'It's good to have friends,' she says. This is where I would normally accuse her of speaking like a *Sesame Street* segment, but today I hold my tongue. She might be talking about me and Nancy, or her and Carla, but either way it seems actually true.

'You've never had that...experience, though?'

'What experience?'

'Like Nancy had. She told you about that? The reason they had to move?'

'Yeah, she told me.'

'You'd tell me if that happened to you?'

'Sure.'

'Okay. It's just that what happened to Nancy was so awful and I'd never want any of my children going through it.'

'Yep.' My fingers ache for the familiar shape of my iPod. I need its weight in my hand. I need a pair of head-phones to block everything out.

'I know you don't like talking about this stuff, but I worry.'

'I know you do. But I'm fine.'

'I'm not talking about psychologists or interventions. I just want to know that you'd come to me if you ever felt bullied or having...dark thoughts.'

'*Dark thoughts*? Jesus, Mum.' My face flushes as I think about the night before, holding the pillow over my face, willing my body to override its safety controls.

164

'Don't be flippant, Clancy. What Nancy went through...That's why she tells someone when she has a problem, and it gets sorted out. Like a trust bridge.'

Oh God, *trust bridge*. This so-called child psychologist came to our school at the start of the year, part of some government program to help struggling TV personalities sell more copies of their books to desperate parents. Mum went to the seminar and came back with nothing more useful than new buzzwords to torment me with. *Trust bridge*, needless to say, was one of them.

'I'm really fine,' I say. 'Really.'

'It's just that you never have any friends over, anything like that.'

'I don't need to have...I've got plenty of friends.' I'm a good enough liar if I keep my voice quiet.

'Anyway, I just want you to know that I'm always here. Whatever's going on. I can listen, or talk, or anything.'

'Thanks. I'll keep it in mind.'

I've had *friends* before, obviously. They were the sort of bright and short primary school allegiances that meant everything in the moment, but not much beyond. And it's all supposed to transform when you get to high school. You're expected to put *play* and *fun* behind you and enter a world where friendship means an intense, hormone-fuelled *connection*. My former friends became all too quickly exactly the type of people I liked the least. It wasn't their shallowness or selfishness exactly, nor their vanity and desperation. It was their acceptance that there was only allowed to be a single type of person, and any variation was something to fear or hate.

'We could invite Reeve over on Sunday,' says Mum.

'For our *traditional* Sunday lunch?'

'It could be nice for you, that's all.'

'Not sure if that's his scene, really.'

'You could invite some of your science friends.'

'God no.'

'I think it would be nice to have other people there, so it's not as daunting for the DeRosas.'

I'm about tell Mum to invite her own friends, but manage to stop myself. 'Fine,' I say. 'I'll ask Reeve.'

'You'll ask him today?'

'Yes. Today.' Reeve and Nancy would probably get along well, but the thought of everyone I like in my house together is stressing me out. Actually, shouldn't we be home by now? I realise too late that Mum's taken a different turn, leading us back through the quiet wide streets in the old part of town. All the well-kept gardens of old people waiting to die, green blooms of watered lawns among the brown stippled nature strips. The dreaded Long Way Home. Designed to allow more time for an inescapable Proper Talk. I sink lower in my seat, like *just wait till I can drive myself around, lady.*

'So,' she says. 'Dad said you talked to him last night.'

'Yeah.'

'I'm not having a go. He really appreciated it. You making him dinner.'

'Oh. Right. Yeah, well I had extra burgers.' I straighten up in my seat. 'He was doing…legal stuff,' I say. 'He had all these papers on the bench.'

'Probably just boring adult paperwork,' Mum says. 'You'd think it would all be done on computers these days, wouldn't you? But there's still all this paper.' She laughs, but it's not convincing.

'Is something going to happen to him?'

Mum doesn't say anything, just narrows her eyes like she's driving through pouring rain.

'Mum?'

'I'm not sure, sweetie. There's a lot of procedures to go through.'

'What do the police say?'

'Not much, to be honest. There's an investigation. They have go through things in a certain way. Nothing to worry about yet.'

Yet.

'What if something happens to him?'

Mum stops the car at an intersection, checks each side of the road twice. The road's empty, but she doesn't move forward. She lowers her head towards the wheel. 'He didn't do anything,' she says, 'so why would anything happen to him?'

'But you can't—' I'm about to argue with her, but the sight of her knuckles, blanched white with pressure, stops me. 'I'm sure everything will turn out okay,' I say.

If I keep my voice quiet, I'm a good enough liar.

By the time we get home, Mum has scrubbed any trace of emotion from her face and the tiny drops of water on the windscreen have turned to steady rain. She switches off the ignition and smiles at herself in the rear-view mirror.

'Here we are, then.' She keeps staring ahead, until I get out. The rain's pretty heavy, so I run to the porch without looking back.

Angus is lying on the old couch with a crocheted rug across his knees. He's reading a busted-up paperback with pictures of pyramids and galaxies on it. I don't have to read the title to know it contains the word *Conspiracy* or *Secret* or *Prophecy*.

'Working hard?'

'Research.' He waves the book at me. *The Hidden Keys of Secret History*. The cover designer clearly fell into a vat of LSD as a child.

'Is that a *unicorn*?'

'Unicorns are a powerful sign in some cultures.'

'They're a powerful sign you're crazy.'

Angus puts the book down. 'How was the first leg of your apology tour?'

My face goes red, betraying me immediately. 'What?'

'Never thought you had the bone density to be a bully.'

'I honestly don't know what you're talking about.'

'She dost protest too much.' Angus laughs. I suspect he's already a few beers down. 'Dad said you had to go and say sorry to some kid you shouted at. Did you really pick on someone at nerd club?'

'It's *doth* protest,' I say. 'The lady doth protest.' A weak comeback at best.

'It's true, isn't it! One day out with Sasha Strickland and you think you're hot shit.'

'Piss off.'

'Language, Clancy.' Mum's teacher voice sounds right behind me.

Angus struggles to tamp down a grin.

'What's going on, then?' says Mum.

'Nothing.'

She narrows her eyes at Angus. 'Nothing?'

Angus does another shrug. 'I was just trying to read.'

'Yep,' I say. 'Great. Obviously everything is always my fault, so why bother to think otherwise?'

Angus pretends to cower under his blanket. 'Don't let her hit me!'

I give it serious consideration. The look of shock on

169

my brother's face would almost be worth it. Instead, I deploy an offended heel-swivel and stalk off.

I'm heading up to my room when I realise I want to email Nancy straight away. Having someone to tell things to is addictive, as it turns out. I go into the kitchen, but of course Titch is on the computer, playing some ridiculous game.

'Are you nearly finished?' I say, channeling a Loving Sister Who Just Doesn't Want You To Ruin Your Mind With Too Much Computer Time.

'No.' His eyes don't move from the screen. His fingers tap on the keyboard seemingly independent of reason. Virtual Titch creeps down a shadowy hallway. 'I'm on here,' he says, blasting away the head of a teeth-baring monster.

'All day?'

'Gotta finish this stage.'

'How long's that going to take?'

Titch shrugs. 'Have to get enough achievements.' He smashes the space bar and a giant spider explodes in a wash of green blood. 'And awards.'

'And then you get your Advanced Diploma?'

'What?'

'Nothing.' I stare at Titch's disgusting unwashed hair, flecked with what I really hope is dandruff. 'When did you last have a shower?'

Titch just grunts. After only a week of parental neglect my brother is devolving into a unicellular organism.

170

Mum comes in, face reset again, like nothing's ever been wrong in history. 'So you'll call Reeve, then?' she says.

'Yes.'

'Yes when?'

'Soon.'

'Today?'

'Yes, today.'

'You've got his number?' Mum gives me what she probably thinks is a knowing mother–daughter look, but comes out like *I've just got lemon juice in my eye.*

'Yes. I'll do it now.'

Titch makes a kissing noise without ever moving his face further than a few centimetres from the computer screen.

Mum's still got the weird half-grin on her face as I walk over and take the phone. Thank God for cordless technology, I think, and then it hits me that I'm a fricking idiot. I could have given Nancy our home number. I could have taken the phone into my room. I really am the absolute worst at making friends. I haven't even got *her* number. And then my mind races ahead and I think of Sasha calling me. I wouldn't want anyone knowing she was on the phone, and I get a little thrill at the thought of it. I bound up the stairs.

The weather's made my room dark and gloomy, the rain tapping against the window. My favourite weather. I find my work pants in the highly organised clump of clothes beside my wardrobe and grab Reeve's business card from the pocket. Angus's old driving manual lies open on my bed where I've left it, dog-eared to hell but mostly memorised. I throw it aside and lie back on my bed, kicking off my boots. I dial Reeve's number and wait, hoping he won't answer.

He picks up, of course, on the third ring.

'Clancy! What is happening?'

'Hello?' I say, because my brain hates me. And then, 'How do you know this is me?'

'What?'

'How did you know this was me calling?'

'I know what your voice sounds like.'

'But...you answered...'

Reeve explodes with laughter. 'Caller ID, Sherlock.'

'Oh,' I say. 'Right.' I hate using the phone. Like, really hate it.

'What's cracking?' Reeve says.

'Are you at work?'

'Yep.'

'How come you're answering your phone, then?'

'Because I'm at work. It's not exactly a hotbed of crime today.'

'What if someone ram-raids Classic Cuts while you're talking to me?'

'It would be Barwen's worst ever case of Skankicide.'

I laugh, but then smack my head, like *Car-crash jokes, Clancy. Just perfect.*

'Anyway,' says Reeve, 'nice to hear from you. How's, you know, everything?'

'Everything's okay.'

'You all holding up? Your family, I mean? My folks send their best.'

No they bloody don't. 'We're getting there,' I say. 'What's new in town? What have I missed?'

'Not much. Dan Cryer locked himself inside the Boystown Raffle car. Said he wasn't getting out until they gave him a thousand tickets. It was pretty funny.'

Dan Cryer is one of the football-playing mouth-breathers that went to school with Angus. 'Surprised he figured out how to open the door in the first place.'

'Or that he knows how many a thousand is.'

'How's Eloise? Business any better?'

Reeve's voice disappears for a second and I hear the unmistakable squeak of food-court chairs. 'Sorry,' he says. Then, 'Thanks,' to someone else.

'I sense donuts.'

The crinkle of a paper bag. 'How dare you,' Reeve says through a mouthful of what I know is plain cinnamon, extra hot.

'How's Eloise, though?'

'Oh, she's great. Well, not *great*, but she's good. Think she's looking forward to you getting back.'

This news fills me with a weird pride. I want to ask Reeve if people still hate me, my family, my name, but I'm too afraid of the answer.

'So listen,' I say. 'The reason I'm calling,' *is that my mother forced me to,* 'is that we're having, like, a lunch here on Sunday. Apparently. I don't know what it is.'

'Okay,' he says. 'It's usually the meal between breakfast and dinner.'

'Sorry. I'm fucking this up. Do you want to come over for lunch on Sunday? I've got a friend—some friends— um, coming over.' This just sounds weird but I press on regardless. 'Anyway, my family will also allegedly be attending, but I will try and convince them not to.'

Reeve laughs. 'What time?'

'Um, lunchtime?'

'Can I bring anything?'

'Just yourself!' I smack myself on the head again. 'Did I just say that?' How do people do this all the time? The invites, the details, the phone calls. It's the actual worst. 'But yes, I don't think you need to bring anything.'

'What's the dress code? Will you provide soup forks, or should I bring my own?'

'You know where you can stick your soup fork.'

'Okay. Looking forward to it!'

We say our goodbyes, and I hang up. This *friends* thing is bloody exhausting.

When Dad rolls up the garage door he's got his old school jumper on. It still fits him, somehow.

'They don't make quality like this anymore,' he says. The same line he uses every time he fetches it from the back of the cupboard.

'It's not *that* cold,' I say.

'Maybe I just felt like wearing it.'

'You felt like smelling of mothballs and itching?'

'You came out here just to critique my fashion sense? What time is it?'

'Couldn't sleep, so I thought I'd visit a weird guy in a shed.'

Dad smiles. He points his thumb behind him. 'Come on, then.'

Inside, everything looks different. All the paperwork is gone from the workbench, and there's a bunch of cardboard boxes stacked against one wall. 'Spring cleaning?' I say.

'Something like that.'

I hear the familiar grumble of the radio. 'We still in the match?'

Dad tips his hand from side to side, like *not really*. 'They've only got to get a hundred and forty-odd. They're none for twenty already.'

'Bugger.' I settle into the bucket seat. I don't even fall out of it straight away now.

'You know what the Aussies need?' Dad says.

I groan.

'They need a raw-boned fast bowler to shake up the top order.'

'You don't say.'

'I've told you about the semi-final, haven't I?'

He has me cornered now. 'Only a few hundred times.'

Back when he played cricket, Dad sometimes filled in for the A-grade team whenever one of their fast bowlers wasn't available. He'd only done it a few times when he got a call one night from the captain. Half the team were down with food poisoning, on the eve of a semi-final against Toowoomba. Just about the biggest match the Barwen team—perennial easybeats that they were—had ever played. He drove up that night and played the next day. Came on first change, and went for twenty runs off two overs. Only given a third because they had no one else to relieve the opening bowlers. Took two wickets in the over, and then another six. He kept bowling until the last batsman was out.

'Eight for seventy-three,' Dad says. 'Fourteen overs, one maiden. Shook them up deluxe.' He moves his hand out in front of him, pushing an invisible cricket ball away down the centre seam. 'Nearly won the game. If it wasn't for our batting lineup, we would've.'

It's a script I can repeat word for word.

'The glory days, they were.'

'Maybe they'll call you up for the next test.'

'Not much use with my back.'

'Once you're better, though. You could reinvent yourself as a crafty spinner.' I rock back and mime a Shane Warne delivery. 'Maybe you could play locally again.'

Dad sits down. 'Think it might be a while before that happens. Not exactly flavour of the month.'

'It'll blow over.'

Dad leans back in his chair, runs his hands through his hair. 'Not from the look of that stuff they sprayed on the house.'

I must give Dad a shocked look, because he adds, 'I know about it, Clance. Bit hard not to, really.'

'Oh. Okay.'

'Thanks for helping your mum clean it up.'

'That's all right.' I don't know what made me think Dad wouldn't have known. 'Did you tell the police about it?'

'No.'

'Why not?'

'It's not worth it, really. In the long run.'

'But they sprayed those...horrible things on the house.'

'Paint comes off.'

'What about my bike, though?'

'Your bike?'

I tell Dad about Angus driving me home. The bogans outside the Cri. *Lightning Lady*, mangled up in the yard.

'I didn't realise, Clance,' he says. 'I honestly didn't know. We'll get you a new one.'

There's a look Dad's had on his face ever since the accident that I haven't been able to place until now. My fearless, stubborn, pig-headed father. He's scared.

This thought frightens me. Dad has always taken things in his stride. Even when his back got so bad he could hardly sit up. Even when the council screwed him with his compo, even when all he was left with was a shitty job with traffic control, he's always been so matter-of-fact about it. Things *will* turn out fine. Everything *will* be okay. Eventually, everyone believed him. Except now, I don't.

He brings his seat back and looks straight at me. 'People aren't always on your side, Clance.'

'Yeah, I know.' Preacher, I think, meet the converted.

'But you can't let them get to you. You'll always know what's right and wrong. *You* will.' Dad pokes me in the shoulder. 'Some people spend their whole lives working that out. God knows I have. You, you've already got it figured out.'

'Have I?'

'Damn right. And it means you've got a head start on everyone else.'

'But I've learned it, you know, from Mum and you. Right and wrong.'

'From your mum, mainly. I've had quite a history of forgetting which is which.'

'Is that why those cops gave you a hard time?'

Dad waves his hand. 'They're just doing their job.'

'But they still think you're...whatever.'

'That's their problem, really.' The voices on the radio rise for a moment, and we both listen in. A wicket. 'Yes! Here comes the collapse,' Dad says, rising out of his chair before grabbing his back and sinking back into his seat. 'So, anyway,' he says. 'How are things with you?'

'I'm okay.'

'With everything, though. Mum says you got into a bit of trouble at work? And at Landsdowne?'

'Just learning right from wrong.' Why's Mum told him about all my crap? I kind of assumed they weren't talking about anything.

'If you need to talk,' he says, 'I'm here. It hasn't been a...very normal couple of weeks. But if anything's worrying you...'

I nod. 'That's what Mum keeps telling me.'

'Well,' he says, 'there's talking to Mum, and then there's talking to me.' He laughs. 'Don't tell her I said that. She'd never let me out here again.'

'What is it about men and sheds, anyway?'

'It's something the female species will never really appreciate,' Dad says. 'It's an eternal bond.'

I roll my eyes. 'Aren't men supposed to create useful things in their sheds? Shouldn't you be building a boat or writing a novel about bullfighting?'

He sighs. 'It's just a little place, I suppose, where I can escape.'

I feel a little sheepish when he says this. I think about the nightly relief when I finally close my bedroom door behind me. I think about the pleasure I take in being allowed to be alone. Maybe we aren't so different.

I glance up at the pinboard on the back wall and it takes me a moment to realise one of the pictures has changed. In the top left corner, there's a small photo of Mum and Dad on their wedding day. I've never seen it before. It's not the formal church-steps portrait that used to be up there, it's a candid shot, two bodies blurred with movement, halfway through turning away from the camera. And they're smiling. Really smiling. The embarrassed and happy grins of two young people trying to escape from a day's attention. The train of Mum's dress is shot through with sun and her hair is mixed up with a crown of purple flowers; Dad's goofy tall-guy stoop looks actually elegant, liberated from a forced pose. His hand rests in the small of Mum's back, one finger curled around the satin trail of a bow. You can tell they're in love.

And, now it's decades of life later. Do they still love each other? Are you allowed not to? Are you allowed to ask? I wonder what Mum thinks of him now. What he thinks of her. I wonder if that's why he comes out here at night, so as not to have the conversation.

'If you…need to talk as well,' I say. 'If you need to tell me anything. I'm, um, here as well.' Sincerity. Always a bad fit.

'Thanks,' Dad says. 'I'll keep it in mind.'

And with that we seem to exhaust anything like a proper conversation. Dad smiles, reaches back and turns up the radio, and we listen together until all my thoughts are blurred together and India hits the winning runs and I'm very nearly asleep.

*I wake up* early, and as soon as my eyes open, my only thought is *Sasha*. Today is the day. The morning, of course, goes so slowly it's like the seconds are dragging themselves through honey. What if we're too late? What if Sasha runs out of patience waiting and thinks it isn't worth hanging around me after all? As soon as Angus gets up I follow him around like a new puppy until he tells me, inevitably, to piss off and wait.

Finally, at half past two, after I've spent hours elaborately overthinking ways in which the day could go wrong, Angus knocks on my door and says he's ready to go. I put on a blouse of Mum's that I've stolen from the line, my cleanest jeans and, regrettably, my one pair of boots.

Hating myself as I do it, I take a bag from the back of my cupboard and unroll the makeup kit Eloise gave me on my first day at work. It's basically untouched. I give myself vampy Cleopatra eyes edged with grey shadow, touch up my brows, smack on dark red lipstick. A little blush to bring out my cheekbones. I swing out the full-length mirror, removing the safety towel. *You fucking sellout*, my brain says to me. *Stylish yet adventurous*, I say back, looking in the mirror, appraising my ridiculous reflection.

I go downstairs and Angus raises an eyebrow but doesn't—for some reason—follow it with an insult. He seems preoccupied with packing his ute with mysterious bags of equipment.

'Got to review the recordings,' he says, as if I care about anything outside of the girl we're about to meet. 'Maybe start a new line of inquiry.' Finally, he throws in Dad's esky. Maybe I'll get a beer, I think. Maybe we all will.

'Just so you know,' Angus says once we're in the ute, 'today is part of an ongoing, serious, scientific experiment.'

'Right-oh.'

'This means we all have to pitch in. I've only invited Sasha because I need all hands on deck.'

'Crystal clear.' I'm actually glad Angus is coming, somehow. Despite myself, I'm well aware Sasha's interest in me could be part of some cruel joke. I've seen enough teen movies to know that people like me are often the playthings of the rich, the bored and the cruel. If Buggs is lying in wait for us, I want Angus to be there too.

When we get to the library carpark the Monaro is there but, thankfully, Buggs is not with it. Sasha's sitting on the bonnet smoking, looking impossibly cool. She's back in black jeans, her eyes ringed with a smoky grey

183

like mine. Needless to say, it looks a thousand times better on her. There's another girl with her, some local skank in an unzipped white hoodie and a too-tight dress the colour of a highlighter pen.

'Who brought the bag of oranges?' says Angus. 'She'd better not be coming as well.'

He needn't worry, because when Sasha sees us she waves and throws her keys to orange-dress girl like *laters* and comes over to where we've parked.

I fold down the middle seat and move onto it but Sasha goes, 'I'm in the middle otherwise I get carsick.'

This is not how it was meant to go. I was meant to be between them, leaning into Sasha on every turn while keeping her physically separated from Angus, whose motives I still haven't quite figured out. I get out and say, 'Hey Sasha,' as coolly as I can, tossing back my hair.

'Hey,' she goes. Then, 'Cool pickup.'

'Cheers,' says Angus, even though she's said *pickup* like an American and Angus is always going on about 'cultural imperialism' like he even knows what he's talking about.

Sasha gets in and shuffles into the middle and I get in next to her and our legs touch. This is good, but it probably means her other leg is touching Angus. As we drive off Sasha waves to the orange girl, who gives us this really dirty look.

Probably jealous, I think. I stare back at her like *she's mine today, bitch.*

We drive out of town and we're going past the observatory and I look out as casual as I can and see that Angus's bike is still there at the bottom of the tower. He doesn't notice it, or at least doesn't say anything.

'So, have you ever seen this beast?' says Sasha. It's the first thing any of us has said for a while. I definitely should have planned some topics.

Angus goes, 'Only in pictures.'

'There's photos of it?'

'Nothing conclusive. There's some good recreations though, from actual witnesses.'

'So it's real, then.'

'The evidence points that way, yeah. At the moment I'm just adding to the knowledge base, but I'm confident it's real.'

'He goes on these internet chatrooms,' I say. 'He talks to all these old pedos about *conspiracies*.'

'I love conspiracies and shit,' says Sasha. 'The moon landing and aliens and whatever.'

'Yeah,' I say, backtracking. 'I guess some of them are pretty interesting.'

'When you find it,' Sasha says, 'are you going to capture it, or what?'

'Maybe,' says Angus, avoiding an actual answer. 'First I want to get video and audio evidence. Once I've got that, I can get some funding for a proper hunt.'

'So where does it live?' Sasha says. 'How do you know where it's going to be?'

Angus chuckles. He slows down and pulls over. 'If I told you that,' he says, 'I'd have to kill you.'

Sasha laughs, but she moves her body slightly towards mine, like *maybe he's serious*. Nice work, Angus I think. Keep it up. Freak her right into my lap.

'It's top secret,' he says. 'Once I get real evidence, people are going to try and beat me to it. All over the world there's going to be cryptozoologists who'll want to be the first to capture it.'

'Cripto-what?'

'Cryptozoologists. Cryptozoology is a parallel science. The study of creatures that have yet to be seen.'

'Wow. That's awesome.'

'It's nice to meet someone around here who believes in what I do. Unlike Clancy.'

'I know where the hideout is,' I say.

'Yeah, and with your sense of direction I don't have anything to worry about.'

Sasha laughs.

'That's not even true,' I say. This is turning into a disaster. My makeup feels like it's sweating off.

'So it's up in the mountains,' says Angus, 'but I can't let you see it.' He pulls out a sleep mask, one of Mum's. It's not a normal lame flimsy one they give you on aeroplanes—like Grandpa used to give us all the time because for some reason he had thousands of them—but has a thick fabric band around the side so you can't even see out the corners of your eyes.

'Ooh, kinky,' says Sasha, taking it from him. She puts it on.

'Do you need any help?' is the best I can come up with.

'Does it work?' says Angus.

'Bloody oath. Can't see shit.'

'That's the idea.'

We drive the rest of the way basically in silence, and I keep stealing glances at Sasha, not convinced the blindfold totally works. I want to wave my hand in front of her face to check, but I don't.

She's got on a black T-shirt for a metal band or something, and it's really tight and I can make out the outline of her bra. My ears are burning hot and I'm still touching her leg with mine, not too much: just enough. My thigh starts to cramp up from holding it so still but I don't move it an inch.

We turn onto the firebreak track and then Angus steers us off and stops the car. Of course he's right: I can't tell if it's the same spot we stopped last time.

We get out and Sasha's like, 'Cool. Feels so *remote*.'

Angus hands us each backpacks and hoists a giant duffel bag over his shoulder.

'What's in here?' I say, willing Angus to admit to more pig's heads.

'Equipment,' he says. 'Essentials.'

We follow him into the bush. I swear it's not the same way we came last time. But then we get to the clearing and there's the hideout. It looks bigger, or something, like he's

187

put more branches on it, or changed the shape.

'Do you stay out here?' says Sasha. She's hugging herself like girls do in horror movies as the killer's sneaking up behind them.

'Sometimes,' says Angus. 'It's really peaceful.'

'It would be, yeah.'

I go, 'If you like leeches crawling up your butt.'

'Piss off, Pantsy. You want to see inside, Sasha?'

'Sure.'

Sasha crawls in and I mouth a version of my brother back to him: *You want to see inside?*

He grins at me and crawls in after her. I give them both double-barrel middle fingers and go in too. There's room for all of us, but only just.

'This is like when I was little,' says Sasha. 'I used to make forts and stuff. Castles. I was a total tomboy.'

'Me too,' I say.

Sasha smiles at me and I feel little Disney birds landing on my shoulders.

'Just gonna check the video,' says Angus, flipping out the viewfinder. He takes a battery out of his bag and replaces the one already in the camera.

'How do you film at night?' says Sasha.

'Night-vision,' says Angus. 'It came with the camera. Got a great deal on it.'

'All that technology,' she says. 'I've got my phone and that's it. Buggs loves that crap though. He gets this magazine that's all about gadgets and shit. It's always got chicks in bikinis on the front, though. I'm like *what do they have to do with gadgets?*'

'Sex sells,' says Angus. 'Where's your man at the moment anyway? Haven't seen him around town.' I wonder if Angus is as apprehensive as me. He is still an Underhill, as much as he tries to convince people otherwise.

'He's been out at Willowbank with his old man, some drag meet. Runs for like a week, but then they stay around after to dick around with the other revheads. I get to keep his car while he's there, though, so...'

'It's a pretty sweet ride.'

'He hates me driving it, but whatever.'

'Your secret's safe with me.' Angus snaps the new battery into place.

'Fuck Buggs, though. He's screwing Courtney, anyway, pretty sure.'

'Courtney Smith?'

'Yeah. Bitch always has that Adidas hoodie on. The white one?'

I wonder if Courtney Smith was the girl Sasha was with at the carpark. She had a white hoodie, but I didn't see if it was Adidas.

'Like Marge Simpson,' says Angus.

'What's that?'

'Always wears the same thing. Probably has a closet full of the same hoodies.'

Sasha hits him on the arm. 'You're *funny.*'

I cough and glare at Angus, but he doesn't notice.

189

That Marge Simpson joke should have been mine. I'm way funnier than him.

'I do what I can with what I have,' he says.

Sasha laughs again. A fake laugh. 'Want a smoke?'

'Sure.' Angus doesn't move from the viewfinder. My mind runs into overdrive. Angus never touches cigarettes. Calls them *multinational cancer sticks*.

'They're in my pocket,' she says. 'You'll have to get them out though, I've got to do up my hair.'

'Hey?' Angus finally unglues himself from the camera.

Sasha nods her head at the pocket of her jeans.

I freeze up. I actually have a feeling like my body's a pile of Jenga blocks and someone's just pulled out the bottom one.

'All right,' says Angus, and sticks his hand in her pocket. He doesn't do it carefully like I did; he sticks his whole hand in there.

'Steady on, soldier,' says Sasha. 'These jeans are expensive.' Then she laughs like he's tickling her.

I want to be sick. I get up and crawl towards the entrance.

'Where you going?' says Angus.

'Out.'

'Out where?'

'I need some air.'

'Hang on a sec, I'm about to bring up the footage.'

'I'll be outside,' I say. 'When your boner goes down you're welcome to join me.' I hear Sasha laugh and it feels

190

sort of good to have scored a point but also kind of awful because of everything else. She's showing off, I think. She's testing me, maybe. Angus will do anything to annoy me, but surely there's no way he knows that I like her, not really. Not in the way I do.

I stand up and breathe as deeply as I can. I try to imagine what it'd be like to live up here in the mountains. The beast, the Big Cat, whatever, would be pretty lonely. It'd have to have a family, though, to have survived this long. It has to have a mate. One story is that a pair of panthers escaped from the circus and fled to the hills. Another one says it's a puma or a lion, brought out here by American troops as a mascot during World War II. Someone like Angus, though, he thinks the beast has always been here. He thinks it's a totally new species, hiding out, waiting to be discovered. If I was the beast, and I'd survived for this long, I'd hope that no one would ever capture me.

I scan the clearing. Part of me wants to run into the hideout and catch them fucking and then scream at them both for breaking my heart and tear down the stupid teepee and stomp on Angus's stupid camera and throw a pig's head at Sasha and then run off into the bush and never have speak to either of them or anyone else again.

The other part of me—the part that's *really* me, knows that I'll just go back to the car and sulk and wait for them to finish and say I'm fine and spend the rest of my life staring out windows and being eaten up slowly by regret.

But then the hideout rustles and Angus comes out.

'Bloody battery didn't even work,' he says. He rummages through the two backpacks Sasha and I brought in, but only pulls out handfuls of electrical cords. 'I got nothing at all last night.'

*Just like every night!* I want to say, right before a raucous studio audience whoops and hollers and I stand there with my hands on my hips: the end of another successful episode of *Sassy Smart Girl Who Actually Is a Big Hit in the Romance Department, Despite What You May Think.* But instead I just shrug at him like *so what?* because it doesn't really matter. He was never going to see anything in that camera anyway.

'I've gotta get something really quick,' he says. 'Stay here, can you?' Before I can answer he bounds off into the bush, leaving me alone in the clearing.

Sasha comes out of the hideout. 'Your brother's pretty intense,' she says.

'That's one word for it.'

'I was just talking to him and he got really angry or something all of a sudden.'

'He *is* a psycho.'

'I just asked him a question and gets all uptight and leaves.'

Fantastic. I knew Angus couldn't remain normal the entire time.

'That...cubbyhouse thing,' says Sasha. 'He actually stays there?'

'Yeah. It's super weird.'

She's rubbing her arms again. 'It's so claustrophobic. I couldn't stand it. I'm cold, are you cold?' She reaches out to touch my arm. 'It's cold, right?' She rubs my arm slightly and I'm suddenly so far from being cold. My brain's going: *do something!* Throwing words at me like *alone* and *forest* and *cold* and *body* and *heat*.

'It's nice though,' I say. 'Sometimes, being just...here.' What the hell did *that* mean? 'We should, um. Sometime...' *We should build a cabin and lie in front of an open fire and never leave.*

'Yeah,' she says. 'The air's nice. Like...newer than in town.'

'I know what you mean.' I look at the goosebumps on her arms, white skin against her black T-shirt.

'I'd like to spend time here,' she says. 'Not, like, *here*, but somewhere out of town. Get away from it all or something, you know?'

My heart tears me up, punching my ribs like a cartoon boxer. 'We should...hang out or something,' I say. 'Some time.' And then I actually flinch, like she's going to attack me.

'Yeah, cool,' she says.

My brain is so set up for rejection, my body so honed to receive disappointment, that I'm already formulating a lame apologetic response to Sasha saying no. It takes me a moment before I go, 'What?'

'I said that'd be cool.'

'Really?'

'Really. We could hang next week. Get a feed or whatever.'

'Oh, sure, yeah. That sounds good.' I'm trying so hard to act like this isn't the single greatest piece of news I've ever received.

'Get some Macca's maybe.' Sasha's talking so matter-of-factly. 'I'll give you a call or whatever.'

'It's a date,' I say, and somehow my voice isn't Disney princess and it doesn't sound desperate. This is the best thing in the history of the world and my heart blooms and not even the sight of Angus returning with a garbage bag in one hand and tent pegs in the other can dampen my spirits. I'd juggle a hundred pig's heads right now. *It's a date*, I think. *It's a date.*

Someone's hammering on my door and I jolt awake, my heart already pounding by the time I've sat up in bed.

'Get up!' says Mum. 'Time to get up!'

'Okay!' I look at the clock and it's already ten. 'Okay.'

I hear her pounding on Angus's door and then Titch's, and she's shouting, 'Is no one in this family awake?' For real, though, she spends half her life lying in bed ignoring us and then razzes us when we sleep in during school holidays.

I get up and run a brush through my hair and—like every morning—my hair refuses the offer. I strike a pose in front of the mirror, which I still haven't re-covered. I mouth *get the Barwen look*, pouting my lips into two botoxed creatures. I push my boobs together but there's no miraculous emergence of cleavage. Still a treefrog in singlet and boxers.

Sasha saw something in me, though. This is the

thought that kept me in a good mood all of yesterday. I helped Angus set up his video camera again without complaint, listened to Titch tell me about the new skating film he wanted to buy, made dinner while Mum and Dad were God knows where. None of it mattered, because I had a date. I keep telling myself not to get too excited, to keep cool. It's not a *date* date, and anyway, why should I care what it is? She's hanging out with me, which I still can't believe.

My work pants are by the door so I throw them on and slip into a comfy jumper and pad down the stairs. Titch is just ahead of me, swaying on his feet, still sleep-drunk, and I pretend to fall on him from behind, grabbing his shoulders so he squeals. We get downstairs and Mum and Dad and Angus are already there, sitting around the dining table, which has been cleared of its usual layer of junkmail. In fact, the whole kitchen is cleaner. Mum's put out coasters and placemats and there's a pot of tea and plunger coffee and a fresh thing of orange juice as well as a heap of toast.

All I can say is, 'Whoa.'

'Sit down,' says Mum. She's got her fake smile on, but her voice is lighter than usual, like she's really trying.

Dad's wearing a new polo shirt, still with shop creases. 'Hi kids,' he says.

I glance at Angus, who just shrugs at me.

I take a seat. We haven't had a breakfast like this in ages, not since Titch's birthday. Usually, everyone just races to eat a bowl of cereal before the milk runs out.

'Coffee,' I say, grabbing a mug. 'The old java. Pappa Joe's Roast. Cuppa char.'

'Just a sec,' says Mum, putting her hand on mine. 'I need to just say something before we start.' She straightens her fork, which already seems straight enough. 'You all know it hasn't been easy this past week, with all that's happened.' She reaches over and squeezes Dad's hand. 'But there's certain things we need to face, to work out together.'

Dad goes, 'I know we haven't all been...the closest recently, but we're still a family. I feel like we've been drifting away from each other lately, and I don't want that to keep happening. There are some things you have to do alone, and some things are better when everyone's together.' He gestures at the table like *you can all start now*.

All us kids put toast on our plates without saying anything. It feels like Mum and Dad are about to tell us they're getting a divorce or one of them's only got a month to live and they're going to say it's not our fault and that they still love us and we'll always have memories to cherish and they're dulling the hurt and years of future therapy with some fried morning food. Nobody even says anything when Titch pours himself a coffee.

'I was involved in an accident recently,' Dad says. 'I tried to deal with it myself. I thought *why would I trouble my family with this?* This just made me sad and it made me angry with myself.' He looks at me. 'I've realised recently how important it is to be there for one other.'

197

Mum dabs at her eye with a tissue, part of the inexhaustible supply that lives in her sleeve, ready to be pulled out like a magician's scarf.

Dad laces his fingers in front of him. I picture him in a courtroom, in the witness stand.

'I was—for God's sake, have some food before it gets cold—I was out on traffic duty. A Wednesday night. Well, a Thursday morning, really. Out on the highway. They're upgrading the lanes, a long stretch, so only one was open.'

He looks over at Titch, who for once seems to be listening.

'It's my responsibility to direct traffic flow coming from town, to tell it when to stop and when to go. It's nearly two in the morning and there's been no cars for an hour. My back's nearly locked up from standing so long.

'I'm...I'm looking up at the sky cause they've moved all the equipment down the road, around the bend, so there's no lights around and the stars...' Dad looks down at his plate. 'I wasn't paying attention. This car comes screaming out of nowhere, it's on me in an instant. But still, I think it's going to slow down. I wave the signal sign at them, like *hey, what are you doing*? but they don't see it or maybe my sign's around the wrong way. I don't know. I don't remember. And then the car's past me and I hear this...*bang*!' Dad slaps his hands together, making us all jump. 'The worst sound. Out there in the middle of nothing and it's like all the thunderclaps you've ever heard, saved up just for this.'

Dad takes Mum's hand again. 'These two kids. Just older than Clance. Just children. The boy, Charlie, he's had his licence for three days. He runs the car straight into the back of a grader. That's a big truck, Titch. Like a really big truck.'

Titch nods. Four slices of toast lie untouched on his plate.

'I tried to help them,' Dad says. 'They'd clipped the grader right on the corner and gone down the embankment. I run over and it's like I can't run fast enough. My back's seizing up as I'm running and then I'm climbing down the slope, trying to get to the drivers side door.'

Dad puts his hands over his face and lets out a big sigh. 'I just want you all to know the story. I want you all to know I did everything I could.'

Angus, next to me, nods his head. 'That's rough, Dad,' he says. 'That's bloody rough.'

Dad goes, 'So people have already said stuff about me. People who don't know anything about what happened have already made up their minds. Some have made their feelings more than clear. I don't want you to listen to any of that. It's bullshit.'

I think about the collection of pink-stained scourers I had to pile into the wheelie bin, the stench of paint thinner coming off them like a cloud.

'I've talked to the police,' says Dad. 'I've told them the truth about everything they've asked.' He rubs his head. 'I will most likely have to go to court.'

'Behind bars?' says Titch, his forehead creased with worry.

'Not behind bars, little man. I just have to tell a judge what happened. I was a witness to the accident. So everyone can know what happened. It's important for my work to know, and the families of the kids. The Jenkes and the Lamaires.'

Jesus, I think. What if one of *us* had died?

'Are you up on, you know, any charges?' says Angus.

Mum gives him a look, but he says, 'What? I want to know.'

'Well, your dad and I talked to a lawyer yesterday,' says Mum. 'She said it will all depend on the families. It's been delayed because of the Jenckes'...beliefs.'

'What beliefs?' says Angus.

Mum goes, 'They're Christian Scientists.'

Normally, this would be where I roll my eyes. Scarfies, we call them, because all the women always tie their hair up with little scarfs. The same white blouses and long skirts. To be honest, though, I was always a bit envious of not having to pick out an outfit every day.

'They have to do certain...examinations before all the details can be worked out,' Mum says. 'So we're not really sure.'

The autopsy, I think. The Jenckes probably didn't want their son's body looked at by doctors. Was that the same religion?

'Anyway,' Mum says brightly. 'We've got Clancy's

friends coming for lunch in a little bit, which will be really lovely.'

Angus gives me a look like *you have friends?* and I mentally credit him a middle finger.

'But I've got to get my Shield Achievement,' says Titch, as if any of us has the first idea what this means.

'We're getting through this as a family,' says Mum. 'And that means doing things together. This lunch will be a lovely chance to meet some new people. That's why I—that's why your dad and I—wanted to get everyone together now. To have a chat.'

'To make sure you were all bloody awake,' says Dad.

'Who's coming?' says Angus.

'Clancy's friend Nancy, her mother Carla and Reeve Lewis, Clancy's friend from work. Is Reeve bringing someone, Clancy?'

'I, uh, don't know.' A tiny sense of dread tickles my stomach. I'd actually forgotten about the lunch. My brain has an annoying habit of removing useful information from its reserves and replacing it with, usually, quotes from *Futurama*. The lunch. Would Nancy and Reeve even get along? *Would* Reeve bring someone? Why hadn't I thought about all this?

Angus mimes a blowjob and I kick him under the table, hard; things returning—briefly—to normal.

'Anyway,' goes Dad, 'this food's getting cold.' He gives a sort of half-grin like *we've still gotta eat*, and we all agree.

*I see Nancy's* mum's car turn into our driveway at eleven-thirty, which seems a little early, but Mum doesn't seem worried.

'That's the time we agreed on,' she says. 'Carla and I.'

We've finished breakfast in usual Underhill formula-one-pitstop time and I'm helping Mum wash up. Angus and Titch have miraculously disappeared in the manner of immediate repulsion that oil and water share with boys and domestic responsibility. Through the kitchen window we both watch the car—which is so clean the sun flashes off it—roll towards us.

'She's bringing an Italian casserole,' says Mum. 'Can't remember the name of it, but she was making it when I talked to her this morning.'

'You talked to her this morning?'

'Yes. That okay?'

'Why wouldn't it be?'

I dry my hands. I don't know why it bothers me that

the two mums have talked before me and Nancy have.

Mum rushes out to the porch to meet them, but I hang back in the doorway. Nancy's mum has a big pot under each arm, lids encased in tinfoil. Nancy sees me and waves, a bunch of red bangles falling to her elbow.

Soon, we're all inside, in the lounge room, which Mum has apparently cleaned as well. She's put cushions over the most obvious stains and draped a throw rug over the side of the chair our old cat scratched to ribbons. We're sitting—mother and daughter—on opposite sides of the room and it's as formal as hell and I already know the Underhills have blown it again. Especially when Dad comes into the room nearly dragging my brothers.

'Hi,' says Dad, trying not to appear like he's literally kneeing Titch in the back to get him through the doorway. 'You must be Nancy, and Nancy's mother?'

Nancy's mum half gets up from her seat. 'Carla,' she says. 'Pleased to meet you. I've heard so much about…' her face shows an instant of social horror. 'All of you. It's great to finally meet you.' Despite an expert recovery, I suddenly like Carla a whole lot more. She has just experienced the tip of the socially awkward iceberg I crash into every day of my life.

'Likewise,' says Dad. I can't pick what's different about him until I realise he's wearing long pants. 'These are the boys,' he says, finally manoeuvering Angus and Titch into the room. The three of them standing side by side is like one of those evolutionary flowcharts.

'Hi,' says Nancy. 'How's it going?'

Angus grunts and Titch sniffs. Better than I'd hoped, really.

We make excruciating small talk for a few minutes. This is not how it was supposed to go. Only a few days ago I couldn't wait to see Nancy and talk to her some more, but now it's like everything has been reset. Thanks, Mum. Let's force two families together just because you want a friend. Just because you want people on your side. When I hear a knock at the door I bolt to get it.

It's weird to see Reeve out of his security uniform. He's wearing a T-shirt and I realise I've never seen his arms uncovered.

'Point me to the keg,' he says. 'Let's get this party started.' He bobs his head behind the flyscreen, his face flickering with the sun behind him.

I open the door. 'Welcome to my humble abode,' I say. 'Don't take any silverware. Not that we have any. It's just, you know, good advice.'

'Duly noted.' Reeve steps inside. 'Who else is here?'

'Just a friend of mine from Nature Club. And her mum.'

'Really?' Reeve has rescued me from conversations with Glenn multiple times at the shopping centre.

'No, she's new. Nancy. You'll like her.'

'Nancy. And Clancy. How fancy.' I make a pained face and he bows. 'Come on, then.'

I have no idea what makes Reeve so confident. He was

in the same class as Angus at school before he dropped out. He never talked about why, but according to Angus both his parents were deadbeats on compo and Reeve had to work to support them. Everyone always assumes they know what sort of person he is because he didn't finish school, but once you knew him, you wouldn't underestimate his intelligence or ambition.

He goes, 'So, Eloise says to say hi.'

'Oh, cool.' I feel like I should have called Eloise, or visited her, but every time I thought about it, I just remembered Raylene McCarthy's face. Eloise doesn't need me hanging around, making things worse.

'She would have come, I'm sure,' says Reeve, who has somehow read my mind, 'but she's gotta work, you know.'

'Yeah.'

Reeve pretends to examine every wall closely. 'Makes sense,' he keeps saying, or 'Just as I thought.' I laugh, but I do actually feel a bit embarrassed that this is the first time he's been to my house.

We go into the living room and I do all the introductions. Mum gets up and gives Reeve a kiss on the cheek, which feels like more affection than she's shown to any of her own children in years. I realise then that today is all about Mum proving how normal our family is, pretending that we act like normal people all the time, that we're not a family of dropkicks and weirdos and murderers. She's campaigning for us, trying to win over one person at a time. This is sort of horrifying, but also sort of endearing.

Once I notice this, I see she's running through a basic phrasebook: *It's been too long. You will give our best to your family, won't you? We should all catch up soon.*

Reeve smiles and nods through the social waltz, but I can tell all his confidence has dried up. He shakes my dad's hand hesitantly and I realise that people probably don't see my dad anymore, they see someone who might have killed some kids.

'Have you got your gun on you, Reeve?' says Titch.

'I don't have a gun, mate.'

'But you're security, right?' Titch mimes a machine gun, shooting it one-handed from his hip. I often worry for the future of humanity, there being a small possibility that tiny psychos like my brother will one day be responsible for not only themselves but also others.

'Not that exciting, I'm afraid,' Reeve says. 'Mostly I walk around and check locks.' He smiles at Carla. He still hasn't sat down, and is playing nervously with his hands.

'You hear about Dan Cryer?' says Angus. 'Locked himself in that raffle car?'

'I was the one who had to get him out.'

'Classic. I heard he pissed his pants.'

'Well!' Mum stands up. 'I should probably get started on a bit of lunch prep. Can you give me a hand, Carla? I don't want to ruin that wonderful casserole.'

Reeve nods at Angus behind Mum's back, using his hands to indicate the extent to which Dan Cryer had wet himself.

Carla gets up and the rest of us realise we're about to be left alone together. 'Did you want to...see my room, Nancy?' I say, deeply embarrassed by the question but pushing through regardless.

'Yeah,' she says. 'Absolutely.'

'Um, Reeve?' I say. I feel like I should include him, but don't know what to say.

'You like dirtbikes?' says Angus, cutting across me.

'Uh, sure,' says Reeve.

'You gotta check this shit out. I've got this DVD with insane tricks.'

'Yeah, definitely.'

Something irks me about Angus hijacking my friend, but I'm so eager to escape I don't really care.

*There's a moment,* as we're walking up the hallway, where I try to mentally catalogue all the potentially shameful details contained in my room. I remember the unmade bed, the numerous items of scattered underwear and the half-finished mug of tea that has been on the windowsill so long it's close to developing a basic system of communication, but when I open the bedroom door, the reality is far worse.

It's only when you look at your bedroom through the eyes of a stranger that you realise it exhibits characteristics you would most closely associate with the lair of a fairy-tale ogre. It's not that my room is dirty, or particularly messy, it's just *all me*. Too much me, too much at once.

Nancy doesn't seem to care, or at least is too nice to say anything. She rolls the chair—mercifully free of rubbish—out from my desk and sits down.

'That was...a little awkward,' she says.

'I reckon.' I sit down on my bed, trying to

casually search for any incriminating food scraps or celebrity biographies. 'I think Mum's been up since 5 am preparing.'

'Tell me about it. Mum made lasagne *and* ravioli. Enough for about twenty people. We don't even have a kitchen in the room so she went to Danny's house to make it.'

'The hotel guy?'

'Yeah. I mean, he's nice, but...' she makes a face.

'Do you think your mum like, *likes* him?'

'I don't even want to think about it. I'd like to see Dad's face, though.'

'Do they still talk? Your mum and dad?'

'Of course they talk. Why wouldn't they?'

'I just thought, since they were separated or whatever.'

Nancy laughs. 'They're not *divorced*!'

'Shit, sorry. I didn't mean—'

'It's fine. It's funny. Dad just gets these contracts overseas. He's an engineer. He's in Dubai helping to build some insane skyscraper. It's only like six months.'

It feels like a disruption, already, in our friendship. 'That must be hard.'

'They're used to it.'

'I mean hard for *you*. Six months is a pretty long time.'

Nancy doesn't respond, just leans forward and picks the driving manual off the floor. 'Cool,' she says. 'You taking your test?'

'Soon. My birthday's December 29, so I have to take it next year.'

'Cool.' Nancy takes off her jumper. It's the first time I've seen her without layers. She's as thin as me, but in a different way. Delicate, maybe. Her head and her hands look bigger in just a tank top. I note with some jealousy the thin strap of a proper bra, and an actual reason for its existence. Everything is proportional, everything is what I am not.

'Awesome,' she says. 'We can cruise the streets together.' She mimes hanging her elbow out a car window. 'The girls at my old school, they were obsessed with boys that had cars. As if owning one meant, like, instant maturity. I can't think of anything worse, though.'

'Yeah. Complete turn-off.'

Nancy gives a smirk. 'What turns you on, then?'

'What? I don't know.' My mouth goes dry. 'Not guys with cars, anyway.'

'So how about Reeve? How does he…fit in?'

My neck flushes red, I can feel it. 'He's a friend. He works at the shopping centre. He's a security guard… but you know that. Um, I work at this makeup place, or I used to work—but I guess I still do—anyway, he works there.'

'Gotcha,' says Nancy, nodding. 'He seems nice. Funny.'

'Really. I'm not, um. We're just mates.' There's no way I can seem believable, especially as uncomfortable and flustered is my default setting.

Nancy's laughing. 'Ooh, a man in uniform, hey?' She jumps across onto the bed. 'Tell me everything!'

Her eyes are green as hell up close, and just like that, we've moved from casual acquaintances to *besties*.

'No,' I say, slightly too forcefully, 'everyone assumes that because I'm a girl and he's a boy and that we hang out sometimes and actually talk to each other that we're suddenly *into* each other.'

'Oh, come on!' Nancy bumps up and down on the bed.

'No, really. It's the worst. I feel like we can't hang out outside of work because people will assume we're *together* or something.'

'You can tell *me*!'

'I'm serious.'

'Go on!' She's shaking her body around like a toddler who's not getting its way. It's pretty annoying. 'Tell me, tell me!'

I go, 'I'm not into guys is the thing,' and it's a few seconds before I realise what I've just said. I want to jump straight back in time three seconds and put a pillow over my face until my stupid mouth stops moving. 'I mean… you know, I'm not…' My useless brain cannot provide me with one more fucking thing to say.

The smile falls from Nancy's face. 'Oh, God,' she says. 'Shit. I'm so sorry.'

'No, it's fine,' I say. It's all a joke, I think. A funny joke.

Nancy pulls her legs up under her. 'I get carried away sometimes. I didn't mean to offend you. I was just trying to be, like, what friends are like. You know. I'm so lame.'

'No, it's fine. I'm not offended. I mean, I don't know

211

what friends do either. I'm not exactly super practised in that area.'

Nancy buries her head in her hands. 'I'm the worst.'

'No you're not.'

Nancy looks up at me, her fingers dragging her cheeks down. 'The worst.' She picks up the driving manual. 'It's like, they should give you one of these, for how to be friends.'

'And then a written test,' I say. 'One I could study for.'

'Exactly. And they wouldn't let you out in the world until you were ready, you know? Until you knew how to do it. And then what to do once you'd made them.'

I lie back on the bed. The familiar smell. The familiar feeling. 'I need a manual for everything, actually.'

'You know,' says Nancy, 'how some people seem to just have it all together? Like, they're just born with all the answers?'

'I hate those people.'

'They're the worst. The rest of us, like, we're just born with the questions.'

Ripping off a band-aid, I think. Diving into the freezing sea. 'I've never told anyone about it,' I say, almost physically forcing out the words. 'About not liking boys. It's just not…and you might not even want to hear about it.'

Nancy turns to me. 'No, I do,' she says. 'I do.'

I grind my wrists into my eyes. 'I don't even know what it is, or what it means. If it means anything. I don't know

212

what it is. I've just always been, you know, the opposite. Of what I'm...supposed to be.'

'You're not *supposed* to be anything. I don't reckon.'

'I don't know. Maybe I haven't been old enough to understand it. But it's like, part of me that I can't even talk about because I don't know what it is.'

Nancy nods.

'And there's a girl I really like. I've liked her ever since I met her. I just...I didn't even know what it meant at first, but I just needed to be around her. And it's love or lust or just another feeling that no one's ever had before. I don't know. I don't even feel like myself when I'm around her. I don't know what to do.'

'You feel what you feel,' Nancy says. 'You can't really stop to wonder about it.'

It's a cliché for a reason: the weight rising off me. Not from my shoulders, but from my chest and my heart. I don't need answers, I just need someone to listen. 'I've always known, I guess. Not *known*, though. Not when I was younger. Just...'

Then my natural panic descends on me, like a lifted sheet settling back to a bed. 'It doesn't matter though. I don't even know why I said anything.'

Nancy lies back so we're side by side on the bed, like we were on her bed, in the motel room. She takes my hand. 'I think this is what friends do, though,' she says. 'I think they listen to each other's problems.'

*A problem shared is a problem halved.* The unfamiliar

213

sensation of one of Mum's sayings finally making sense. 'I thought you said you hadn't read the manual.'

'Maybe we should write it.'

Nancy's here, and listening. Just that is the best thing ever in the world. And not even Titch bursting in, without knocking, to say lunch is ready can ruin it.

*The table is* fuller than I've ever seen it. The napkins and placemats from this morning were, of course, set out for lunch. Carla's lasagne and ravioli look amazing. Mum's made a pile of sandwiches, and there's cheese and crackers, even Cheezels for Titch, whose strict personal diet precludes all foods that can't stain your skin.

Reeve is deep in conversation with Angus. They're huddled over Reeve's phone sniggering at something. I always forget they were in the same grade. They've always been so separate in my mind, but here they are, laughing and joking around like pals. This is the male version of friendship, maybe. One boy shows the other a video of a motorbike ramming someone's testicles and thus a life-long bond is formed.

Mum comes from the kitchen with potato salad, Carla close behind. 'Everybody here?' she says.

'Think so,' says Dad.

We all take our seats around the table, and it's surreal

to be so surrounded by people in my house.

'This is lovely.' Mum's inevitable line. 'Eat,' she says. 'Eat!'

And it's all going well until—mid mouthful—I hear the crunch of gravel in our driveway. Dad's sitting opposite me and he looks up, a strange shocked look in his eyes. A ripple of panic shudders through me at Dad's expression.

Titch runs to the window. 'It's an orange car,' he says. He whistles like Angus does and goes, 'Sweet ride.'

There's the sound of a car horn, and suddenly it all clicks. Shitting hell. Please, no.

'Whose car's that?' says Dad, but I'm already up from the table, paper napkin hanging from my pants. I rush to the window and of course it's the Monaro. I see Sasha's hand waving from the drivers side window. She was supposed to *call*. Our date was supposed to be *next* week. She beeps the horn again, holding it down way too long.

Mum goes, 'Who is it?'

'No one,' I say. 'Just a friend.'

'Oh,' she says. 'Someone else? You should have told me.'

'No, they're not coming in.' Oh God. The lunch. Sasha. Why the hell does this stuff always happen? 'I think I might have to go,' I say.

'You've hardly started your lunch.'

'I'll just, um....' Bloody shitting hell. There is no way anyone can know who it is.

Mum goes, 'We've got guests.'

'This is a *family* meal, Clancy,' I hear Dad say. 'I'll come out with you.'

'No! No, it's fine.' I don't want to turn around. I can't. I squish my feet into my boots that I've left by the door, steal Angus's aviators from the pocket of his jacket. 'I'm sorry,' I say. 'This is important.'

The Monaro's horn goes again. For crapping crap's sake. I peer through the flyscreen to make sure Sasha isn't reversing away.

Mum unleashes her most serious teacher voice. 'Clancy, that's enough. Your friend will have to wait.'

Now or never. I open the flyscreen and run out, tripping down the stairs in my half-on shoes.

'Clancy!' Dad's voice roars behind me.

I trot up the driveway to the Monaro, acting as casual as I can and open the passenger door, as if this is what we've planned all along, as if I haven't just broken my parents' hearts and stood up my only two friends. I'll tell her we can't meet today. I'll explain that she should have called, that she shouldn't just turn up unannounced and expect me to drop everything.

She smiles at me with her tiny, pretty teeth. 'Hey,' she says. 'You gotta tell me where you got those boots. They're totally sick.'

And so I giggle like a weirdo. And so I get into the car. And so I fall immediately and hopelessly in love.

Sasha reverses back up the driveway, and I see Dad's stooping frame in the doorway and he's shielding his eyes, trying to recognise the car. I slink back in the seat and close my eyes.

The best way to approach this, I tell myself, is just to keep looking forward. I try to conjure up my own affirming slogan. *If You Look Back You'll Never Win the Steps You Never Take.* I tell myself there's nothing I can do about what's happened. I've done it. I've disappointed my parents, wrecked my friendships with Nancy and Reeve, all to spend an unspecified amount of time doing an unspecified thing with a girl whose boyfriend most likely sprayed *MURDRER* across our house. That old story. We'll all look back on this one day and laugh. Though whether with me or at me, I'm not entirely sure.

We're driving away, fast, from the scene of my betrayal, and I'm trying to stop my hands from shaking. My shoes are *totally sick*. Maybe I don't look as shit as I think I do. Maybe I've just spent my life perfecting the messy, just-woken-up look. Maybe I'm fashion-forward, maybe worn out work pants and a jumper that used to belong to your dad that says *Superstars of Sailing* is what everyone will be wearing next season. I pat down my pockets and find Reeve's business card and Mum's fifty-dollar note.

Sasha, for her part, doesn't seem to notice that I'm swirling in a moral typhoon. In fact, she starts talking as if we've been chatting for the past hour. 'So I get home yesterday,' she says, 'and there's this message from Buggs saying that he's going up the coast with his dad and that.'

There's a pause, where it's clear I'm supposed to say

218

something to this. Maybe we *had* been talking longer. I've just been staring at her jawline, admiring how it sweeps up like a perfect wave. How do girls like this even *exist*? If I had Sasha's looks, I'd spend all day in front of a mirror.

'No way,' I say.

'Yeah, and he doesn't even ask if it's okay. His uncle's got this sort of shack up there, right on the water, bought it in the sixties, and now it's, like *prime* real estate. All these million-dollar mansions around it and it's just this shitty old beach house. It's so foul.'

I'm not sure whether Sasha is talking about the state of the house, or the unclaimed profits, but either way I murmur agreement.

'He's such a dick sometimes.' Sasha strikes the butt of her wrist on the steering wheel. 'Don't know why I put up with his shit. He's probably got some sandy-vag Gold Coast bitch on speed-dial anyway.'

'Yeah,' I say. 'That's not good.' Any guilt about running away from the lunch table is quickly vanishing. *Break up with him*, I think, with all my effort. *Breakupwithhimbreakupwithhim.*

'Anyway,' she says. 'Today is just about us, Clancy.' She reaches over and touches my arm with her cool, soft fingers. 'Hey, check it out.'

She reaches over me and I actually jump with fright but she just opens the glovebox. A bottle of Jack Daniels. 'It's some special edition shit. He thinks I don't know about it. He thinks if he puts it in a plastic bag at the back of his kitchen cupboard I won't find it. Fucken idiot. Probably saving it up for the day he works out how to suck his own cock.'

My mouth dries up. Whiskey with Sasha. This is *right*. This is the grown-up, black-and-white movie stuff our life should have. I'll take up smoking and sit on some high-up apartment window ledge, looking out over a real city. We'll drink liquor from the bottle and only ever wear oversized men's shirts.

We pull into Macca's and Sasha turns into the drive-thru. She orders three apple pies and a Diet Coke and I get a cheeseburger meal. At the drive-thru window, Sasha goes, 'Hey, bitch,' and when I lean over to look up at the window I see it's the girl from the carpark. She has a hoodie draped over the top of her uniform, all white save the tiny blue Adidas logo. Her name-tag says *Courtney*.

'What's up, Sash?' she says. 'I knew it was you because of your order.'

*Sash*. Could I call her *Sash*? It sounds kind of wrong.

'Make sure the pies are extra hot,' Sasha says. 'No ice in the Coke.' Then, 'You know Clancy, right?' She leans back in her seat so Courtney can see me.

Courtney looks at me briefly, like I'm something she's found under her shoe. To Sasha she goes, 'You going to Jase's party?'

Sasha's like, 'Maybe. Depends what we're doing later. Clance is, like, super fun. We go on adventures.' *Clance*, I think. *Clance!* Take that, bitch.

Courtney makes a snorting noise. 'Whatever. You wanna upsize?'

'Yeah,' says Sasha. 'That way we can share the chips.' She turns to me and sticks her tongue out.

I laugh stupidly and hand her Mum's fifty. Screw new shoes, this is worth it.

'Got anything smaller?' says Courtney.

'Your dad's dick?' says Sasha.

Courtney gives her this look, like *I can't even*.

I really hope Courtney is screwing Buggs, although if he does actually have two girls willing to voluntarily spend time with him then the universe really is a cruel and merciless void.

We get our food and Sasha rolls the car around to the carpark. 'Want to go anywhere?' she says. She revs the engine and for the first time I can see the appeal of doing this. It's kind of thrilling. The afternoons I spent at the skate park were full of these sounds, the impossible animal volume of engines and car stereos, those mutant bumps and thrums.

'I know a place,' I say. 'It'll be perfect.'

'Another adventure,' says Sasha. 'I love it!' She guns the engine again and we squeal out of the carpark. It's terrifying and it's weird and it's fucking amazing.

*Through the aviators,* through the burny buzz of whiskey, the world is a nice greyish blue. We've got our feet up on the railing, baking in the weak sun. We're above the world and perfectly alone. We're adults. Long legs and warm backs and endless possibilities. Atop the observatory, the place we first met.

'So what do you want to do with, like, your life?' I say, watching a patchy cloud slowly dissolve. I'm so full of fast food, and so mouth-fumblingly tipsy, but so very happy.

Sasha laughs. 'That's a deep question.'

'Do you think you'll stay here, though? Like, in Barwen, with your job, or Buggs, or...' A line of questioning I've been practising over and over in my head.

'Probably not. The job's okay, but I can work in a travel agent anywhere. It'll probably be easier somewhere else, really. Won't have my mum as my boss.'

'I guess everyone likes to travel.'

'Exactly.'

'What about your family, or whoever? Would you stick around for them?'

Sasha lifts one leg off the railing and rolls her foot around. 'I've got Mum, but that's it. She's never going to leave.'

'And Buggs?' I say, subtle as a hammer. 'Does he want to travel?'

'He wouldn't last a second outside Barwen. His family practically owns everything so why would he want to move? As long as I stay here, I'm stuck with him.' Sasha takes a swig of the Jack Daniels, slams it back down on the metal floor with a clang.

'Yeah,' I say. 'I guess.' I take a slug of whiskey as well, a big, match-strike mouthful that hurts all the way to my stomach.

She rolls onto her side, so she's facing me, so I can almost feel her. 'Fuck it, though,' she says. 'Fuck him and his family. I'm going to move to Brisbane or probably Sydney. I've got friends who are, like, full-on models. I'll probably stay with them. They're always asking me to come down. Saying *I* could be a model or whatever. What do you reckon?'

'Definitely,' I say. Two breaths, and I roll over to face her. 'You could definitely be a model.' There's a tiny clump of mascara on one eyelash.

'Yeah. I'll probably stay for Christmas and then piss off. Can you imagine people's faces, like, if I just didn't tell anyone and then just left? It'd be classic.'

'For sure.' I picture us flying down the highway in the Monaro, the road disappearing either side of us. Driving wherever we wanted to.

Sasha says, 'I'd want to have New Year's in Sydney, though. My mate's got this apartment *right* near the bridge. It'll be amazing. The fireworks are so shit in Barwen.'

'Yeah,' I say. Then, 'My birthday's just before New Year's. The twenty-ninth.'

'Really? You should *totally* come down. It's going to be *massive*.'

I sort of scrunch up my face. 'Really? I could come?'

'Yeah, totally. It's going to be amazing. You're cool. You can watch me take the world by storm.'

This is our new life, I think. This is my ticket out of here. Sasha, Sydney, models, *huge*. I've got money saved up, my car money, but I won't need a car now. Sasha and me. We can make it work. 'Sounds great,' I say. 'Sounds the best.'

Sasha sticks her tongue out at me like *Rock and Roll!* and her face is so close to mine that I notice again the tiny row of blonde hairs above the dark line of her eyebrow. She looks at me with her wide eyes and smiles, just slightly and my heart shoots fireworks because she's daring me to move closer and then my brain says *Happy Birthday, Clancy* and I lean in and close my eyes just before my lips brush hers and they're soft and her bottom lip is *so soft* and I push against it. She makes a quiet noise and I feel her mouth open against mine. My fingers move so close to her gorgeous hair but then I can't feel it. I open my eyes and Sasha's pulling her head back.

'No,' she says. 'I...' then she puts her hand on her mouth. 'What the *fuck?* She sits up. 'What the *fuck?*'

It takes me a second to realise what's going on and for a wonderful moment I think she's talking about something else, like she's seen a shooting star or it's suddenly started raining or she's just remembered something important, or—

'Did you just try and *kiss* me?!' Her eyes are huge and round and she stands up saying 'You...' and she holds her hands out either side of her like she's trying to stop two walls from closing in.

Panic pummels me like falling boulders and I say, 'I'm sorry, I thought you...' She kissed me back, didn't she? 'I'm so sorry. I'm *so* sorry. I didn't mean to.' My voice is coming out rapid-fire and my heartbeat's matching it. 'I don't know what I was thinking.' You stupid bloody idiot, Clancy.

Sasha's pointing at me. 'Are you queer?' she says. 'Are you fucking queer? Oh my God.' I don't say anything and then she laughs. 'You *are*, aren't you? Oh my fucking God. You're a little fag!'

'I'm not,' I say. 'I'm not. I didn't mean to.'

'You *are*.' Sasha runs her hands through her hair. 'Fuck. Me.' She taps her finger against her head. 'This makes a *lot* of sense. Fits right in with your fucking psycho family.'

'We're not psycho.'

225

Sasha's laughing hard now, like she can't hold it together. 'I knew it. I knew you were. All you Underhills are fucking crazy.'

I realise I'm still lying down and somehow this makes me angrier than anything, like she hasn't even given me a chance. 'I'm not a *queer*,' I say, standing up. 'I'm not anything.' I step towards her, my head a ball of white-hot embarrassment and rage. 'You don't know a fucking *thing*!'

'You going to push me off the edge?' she says. 'You gonna kill me? Gonna be just like your dad?'

And oh God I *do* want to kill her, I picture the pewter dragon knife in my hand and I'm stabbing her right in the soft hollow of her neck, watching the blade going in through her skin and not even feeling it. But then I realise there's no blood and the knife isn't slicing it's erasing, it's just leaving an absence behind. And it's not her neck I'm imagining, it's mine. I'm running the blade across my throat and it's so beautiful, so absolutely peaceful, like when you wake up from a nightmare and remember none of it's real.

I slump down on the platform. I'm crying like a lunatic before I realise it and I can't catch my breath and then I'm curled up in a ball and I smell dirt and the heat from the sun that's still held in the metal. I hear Sasha's footsteps behind me and then she's climbing down the stairs, each footfall like a clanging bell, all the way down. The car starts up, revs and takes off.

I lie there for I don't know how long, like if I never move again, nothing bad can happen. I just want to stay here, curled up like this until my mind stops working or the world ends or preferably both. I *am* a fucking idiot. I *am* a fucking psycho. I *am* a fucking queer. Why did I ever think she actually liked me? I think of all the things I did around her, the way I fucking *acted*, and I curl myself up even tighter. I can't show my face in town ever again. Or at school. *Fuck*. School.

I squeeze my eyes closed. All the years I've spent making myself as unremarkable as possible, flying under the radar, giving no one—no one—a reason to single me out or notice me. This is how I survived. I wasn't a girl, I wasn't an Underhill, I wasn't a faggot, I wasn't anything but another face to ignore. I've been teased before—hasn't everyone?—but it was just scattergun schoolyard prejudice. Now it's real. They've got me. It's all going to change, and I can't go back. I just can't. Sasha will tell everybody. Mum and Dad's face when they find out. Angus, Reeve, everybody. *Nancy*. She said it was okay. She said I could talk about it. Lying bitch. My crying turns to sobbing turns to howling and I'm a wounded animal, I'm the Beast of Barwen, lying here thrashing in my own misery.

When I'm finally spent, when I'm just mucus and two dry eyes, I roll onto my back. Cartoon clouds above me. I think, *How is it that everyone else works out who you are before you do?* I'm sized up, figured out, drawn over and boxed in on all sides. There's a red ant crawling towards my face so I sit up. The bottle of Jack Daniels is still there. I grab it and get to my feet.

I lean over the railing. It's a disgustingly clear afternoon, the whole world out there waiting for me in high definition. There's no way I'm letting it make me a part of it. I hold the bottle over the edge, releasing my grip bit by bit until it slips from my grasp and I feel a jolt of adrenaline. I hear the bottle smash and look down at the wet starburst pattern, the glitters of glass. Then I lean myself over the edge. I lean over until my body starts to tell me I've gone too far and I hold it there.

The ground is just dust and rocks and I don't like the idea of landing on it which is strange because it shouldn't really matter. I want it—somehow—to be water. I don't want resistance. I want it to accept me and pull me under and run me below the current and lead me away to another place. I close my eyes and lean out further, reaching my hands out in front of me, feeling the pleasant sensation of my weight shifting from my feet all the way to my head.

𝐴 𝒆𝒂𝒓 𝒉𝒐𝒓𝒏 beeps and my body jolts. I snap my eyes open and before I realise it my reflexes kick in and my arms shoot back to grab the railing. I'm further over the edge than I've thought, practically balancing on the rail. My stomach lurches as I try to regain my balance. The aviators slip off my nose and fall towards the dirt. They hit the ground and both lenses pop out. My pulse thumps at my temples. I need to stay still and there's a breeze ruffling my clothes and I will it to stop, *please just calm the fuck down*. The horn beeps again but I have to concentrate. I have to slowly and deliberately shift my weight backwards. My arms tremble as I work back over my balance point and then I kick my legs in the air behind me until finally I fall back and I'm crouching behind the safety of the railing. It's like I can't breathe fast enough to catch up with myself. Adrenaline surges through me.

'Pantsy, you nutjob!' I hear Angus's feet on the stairs.

I rub my eyes and wipe my nose on the sleeve of my jumper. My eyes are still puffy but there's nothing I can do about them. What am I going to do, anyway—pretend I accidentally nearly fell off the tower?

Angus runs at me and grabs my arm like I'm going to throw myself off again. 'What the hell were you doing?' His face is red and his eyes dart back and forth between mine.

I shrug.

'You could've killed yourself.'

'That was kind of the idea.'

'What?' He grips my arm tighter. 'Jesus, Clance. Jesus.'

'It's fine,' I say. 'I'm over it now.' I'm talking in this sort of weird flat tone, like it's not really my voice that's coming out.

'Let's go back,' he says. 'I can drive you home.'

'I'm fine up here.'

'No. You're not.'

'Can you…can you just give me a minute? Can you let go of my arm?'

'Not really, no.' Angus is squatting down, swivelling on the balls of his feet like he's waiting to spring into action.

I take a huge breath and let it out. 'Dude, it's okay. I'm not going to do anything stupid.'

'You promise?'

I nod, like *come on already*. He lets go of my arm and I slump back against the railing.

Angus sits down as well, but won't stop staring at me. 'What's going on?' he says eventually. 'Is it Dad's stuff?'

I nod. 'Yeah. But...'

'What is it, then?'

Fuck it. 'It's Sasha.'

'Oh. Shit. Wait, did someone hurt you? Was Buggs here?' Angus looks around wildly, as if someone's going to run up the stairs behind us.

'No,' I say. 'Nothing like that. I was just really, really stupid.' I can't even bear to think about it. I keep replaying the moment I kissed her. I keep thinking *If only you'd held back*.

'But she said something to you?'

I nod. I'm so sick of talking.

'Listen, Clance. Sasha's an idiot. When you let *Buggs*... you know, your judgement's clearly not the best.'

My arms start shivering, and I can't stop them.

'You like her,' he says. 'Don't you?'

I nod again.

'She's not worth your time, Clance. Seriously.'

He's right. Of course he's right. What does that make *me* though? I spent so much time working out ways to impress her. She's probably on the phone to Buggs already. *FAG* is easier to spell than *MURDERER*.

'Angus,' I say, 'I told her stuff.'

'What sort of stuff?'

'Stuff about Dad. About our family and everything.' I start to feel tears.

231

'Aw, who gives a shit, really?' he says. 'Everyone's already made up their minds.'

'I tried...' The tears are fat and heavy on my cheeks. 'I tried to kiss her.' It feels even worse when I say it out loud.

'Okay.' Angus doesn't say anything more, just moves closer to me so our shoulders touch.

'I'm such a fucking idiot.'

He hands me a hanky. 'It's clean,' he says. 'Mum bleached the living hell out of it. I never use it because I'm a real man.'

In that moment, I love my stupid brother. 'I tried to kiss her,' I say again. 'I thought she wanted to, but she flipped out and said I was a faggot, and Dad was a psycho, and that all of us were...' I break down. I cry into the hanky, which smells like fresh laundry, the same geranium detergent Mum's used all my life. It's such a fucking wonderful smell.

'Sasha's a dickhead,' says Angus, rubbing my back. 'Her and Buggs and all the other dropkicks around here. That's all they've got. Rumours and gossip. All that shit. Got nothing else going on in their lives.' He lets me cry for a little longer. Gives me time.

'Why did I think she'd want to hang out with me?' I say. 'Why did she even want to?'

'Like I say, she's got nothing else. Probably gets off on the drama. Stupid little bitch.'

A tiny part of me still wants to defend her, and I don't know why. 'So you don't, like, *like* her?'

'Sasha? As if.'

'But, at the hideout?'

'I was just dicking around. But c'mon, *Sasha*? All that fake emo bullshit? I've met *uni* girls, man. She's got nothing on them. They're real women.'

'Gross.'

'You say that now, but when you get out of this dump, when you're at whatever uni you pick or whatever country you end up in, hoo-boy!' he fans himself like a southern belle.

'Piss off. I'm not going anywhere.'

'Hell you are. You're the smartest person I know. Few years time, you're going to be knee-deep in puss.'

'Fucken perv.' I knock his arm off me. 'Gross.'

Angus laughs. He says, 'Whatever it is you want to be being knee-deep in, you'll have it.'

'You're so foul.'

He stands up, smiling, holding out his hand so he can pull me up. 'Listen,' he says. 'One day all of this shit,' he spins his finger around his head like, *take it all in*, 'you won't even think about. You're going to be out there doing something amazing while the rest of us are still stuck in our crappy hometowns trying to figure out what we're doing with our lives.'

'But I don't know what I'm going to do. I'm just some loser. Oh Christ, everyone's going to know about it.'

'Anyone who thinks they know who you are, anyone who's judging you—just means they've got nothing worthwhile in their own lives. People like Sasha, they're going to be stuck here forever.'

'She's going to Sydney,' I say. 'She's got friends who are models. One of them has an apartment near the harbour bridge. She could *be* a model.'

Angus makes a face like *der, Fred* and smacks himself on the forehead. 'Load of bull. She was in the grade below me, man. Dumb as dogshit. Always making shit up. Only reason she's got a job is cause her mum owns the travel agent's. That's some heavy irony. Barwen's as far as she's travelling.'

I squint out at the mountains, a graph of light blue in the distance. Maybe he's right. 'You're pretty wise for a massive douche.'

'I've been sixteen,' says Angus. 'That's all.'

'Thanks, anyway.' An awkward moment of real emotion passes between us. First time for everything.

Angus goes, 'Want me to take you home?'

I wipe my eyes. I remember the lunch. 'Not really. Is Dad steaming?'

'He'll be fine. He sort of ran up the driveway and Mum had to go get him.'

'Shit. What about Nancy and her mum?'

Angus shrugs. 'They'll live. They stuck around to eat. Reeve, too. He's a good guy. Kept the conversation going. You got me out of staying, though. Said I'd go and find you.'

'Can you not find me for another few years, then?

Maybe leave it until Mum and Dad are both senile and can't remember who I am?'

'Yeah, all right,' Angus says. 'I'm sure I could take a little longer.' He rubs his chin. 'I do have to change the tape at the hideout. Pretty sure I've figured out what's been going wrong.'

'Really think the beast has put in an appearance in the last twenty-four hours?'

'Only one way to find out.'

I sigh. 'And you call *me* a nutcase.'

'Who was it about to throw themselves off the tower half a second ago?'

'Fuck off.'

'Whose brother saved whose life?'

'Get your hand off it. I was fine.'

'You can keep my hanky, by the way. But don't think I don't know you took my sunnies.'

I shake my head. Our relationship has regained its usual rhythms. Which is excellent. 'Lead on, Dr Phil,' I say.

We don't say much as we drive up to the hideout. We've both got questions, probably, but silence is fine by me. I watch the scenery go past the passenger window with my head propped up on my hand. I'm trying to convince myself that this past week has been all a dream, that I'll wake up back to my boring life, which I will now obviously value as I should and treasure forever. It's not a dream, of course. The trees are real trees. The grass moves too convincingly in the wind. It's not a fairy tale, or at least not the good kind. At some point soon I'll have to face a crowd of Barwenites holding pitchforks and flaming torches.

'Sure you're okay to head up?' says Angus. 'You still look a little pale.'

'I'm fine,' I say, sounding far from it.

'Just checking.' There's a tiny trace of concern in my brother's voice, a rare inflection.

And when Angus stops the car, he doesn't throw bags

at me or shout. He just grabs one backpack and jerks his thumb over his shoulder like *come on, then.* He doesn't run off ahead. Instead, he walks beside me, staring up into the canopy of trees. The first spits of rain.

I'm just wondering how much longer we've got to walk when Angus stops. He peers through the tall grass like a hunter. The clearing is just ahead of us.

'Oh, shit.' He turns back and gestures me forward. 'Clancy, check it out!'

I look where he's pointing, but only see the same patch of grass, the same weird hideout, the same glint of metal tent pegs. 'What?'

'Look!' He creeps forward into the clearing and I follow him. He puts down the packs and crouches down near a divot in the grass. He puts his hand to his cheek. 'The pig's head,' he says. 'I tied it down right here.' He points to the ground, at some upturned dirt where a bunch of pegs are lying on their sides. 'Holy shit.' Then, suddenly: 'The camera!' He gets up and strides towards the hideout.

I stare at the tent pegs for a moment. *No*, I tell myself. *Something's just taken the pig's head. Something normal.* I don't want to follow Angus into the hideout, that would just be admitting I'm interested. But of course I follow him.

We go in together, and the first thing I notice is that the tripod's been knocked over and the camera's fallen off it.

'No, no, no, no,' goes Angus. 'What are you doing to

me?' He picks up the camera like it's a newborn kitten and swivels out the viewfinder. After a moment, the screen lights up. 'Oh yes,' he says. 'Thank you baby Jesus.' He hugs it to his chest. 'Wait. Clancy, hold this.'

He gives me the camera and goes over to the digital recorder, which doesn't seem to have moved. 'Yes,' he says. 'Yes yes *yes*. This is great.'

Even I have to admit to myself I'm a little excited. As much as every rational part of my brain knows there's no way the Beast of Barwen could possibly exist, some tiny part of me suddenly and desperately wants it to.

We huddle around the little screen as Angus plays back the tape. He scrubs it forward and we see the clearing, basically unchanged from, I guess, yesterday morning. It's like a time lapse on a nature doco: quick rustles of leaves and grass the only real movement. The shadows lengthen and the camera flicks over to night-vision. *Jesus*, I think, *how much did this set-up cost?* All the while the dark shape of the pig's head remains in the bottom left corner. It's daylight again: this morning. Angus chants under his breath: 'Come on, come on, come on.'

And then the screen goes blurry, just for an instant, and then back to the clearing. Angus slows the tape down. The pig's head is gone. I get a chill. 'Holy shit,' he says. 'Ho. Lee. Shit.'

He rewinds the tape, back past the dark flash, and pauses it. He gets me to read out the time-code and he fiddles with the audio recorder until it's ready. He's not saying anything, just breathing really fast.

He presses play and we're watching the clearing again, this time with sound synched up, just the rustle of wind, the occasional bird cry. I hardly want to watch. A few minutes pass and I go to ask *how long* but he shushes me with his hand.

It's the sound we hear first. A huffing noise: deep, quick nostril breaths.

I put my hand over my mouth.

A loud grunt.

Then a scratching noise like a sudden gust of wind and the image shakes and a bunch of leaves falls over the camera. Then the breaths again, getting softer.

'The fuck?' Angus pulls the viewfinder up to his face but I wrench it back down so I can see it too. The leaves fall away and we can see the clearing again, but tilted on a slight angle. The pig's head is definitely gone. The image starts to teeter and then it falls and it's a closeup of Angus's sleeping bag.

'Oh my God,' I say. 'What happened?'

Angus rewinds the tape and watches it again, slowing down the part where the leaves obscure the view. He squints at the viewfinder. 'Shit. You can't see anything. But it was *definitely* the beast, right? You heard it, right?'

'I heard *something*.' The weird sound of its breath. Whatever it was must have knocked the camera over.

'Okay,' says Angus. 'Okay.' He's making hand movements, like he can't decide what to do next. 'Okay, we've

239

gotta go.' He scrambles out of the hideout. I'm not sure what to do but he sticks his head back and shouts 'Come on!'

I follow him out and he's crouched over the place where the pig's head was. A misty rain traces my face. 'It wasn't here that long ago,' he says. 'We've got to track it.' He picks up his backpack.

'Track it?'

Angus squints at me. 'You can't chicken out.'

'I'm not chickening out,' I say, even though I totally am.

'This could be *huge*. Right? Right?'

'Yeah, fine.' Part of me *does* want to know what's going on, even though the whole situation is super creepy.

'Just stay close to me,' Angus says. 'Watch your feet and follow me.' He leaps off into the bush and I jog after him, not wanting to be left behind.

The rain starts falling more heavily, slapping the leaves and the grass. I have to call out to Angus, who's bounding ahead. 'What are we going to do if we find it?'

'Get a photograph.' He slaps his backpack. 'Camera in here. Been wanting to use it forever. A great scientist is always prepared. I've got it preset for action shots, so even if it's moving...' He stops and crouches down.

'What?'

'Look.' He points at the ground where there's an indentation in the grass, a hollow the size of a dinner plate. Angus makes a movement with his hand like *pawprint*. I stare at the ground, trying to imagine a creature leaving its mark. It could've just been a natural depression. But then Angus points up ahead, grinning. I follow his finger and there's a broken branch hanging off a nearby tree.

'It could've just snapped off by itself,' I say, hardly even convincing myself.

'Look at the *way* it's snapped though.' Angus goes over to the tree. 'See how it's twisted like that? I've seen this sort of thing online.' He thrusts his hands into his pockets. 'It's a tell-tale sign.' The rain's plastered his hair down so it's gone darker and he looks so much like Dad in those photos, just missing the motorbike.

I shrug. The rain's getting really heavy now. 'Can we come back?' I say. 'Can we get jackets and torches or whatever and come back?'

'No way,' he says. 'We're *tracking* it. Time is of the essence. We can buy hundreds of jackets with the money I'll get from this photo.'

'The money *we'll* get.' I feel water seeping into my left shoe. I look down and the tips of my boots are black and soft. 'And you're buying me new shoes.'

'Okay, whatever,' he says. 'But we gotta keep going.' He moves away, keeping his body close to the ground so he's waddling, even though there's no real reason to do so.

I follow him for maybe five minutes and we're heading down a slope with the rain hammering and my hair's hanging down over my eyes and I keep slipping on wet leaves. Angus stays in front, every so often bending down to analyse some invisible clue on the ground or stopping to examine leaves on a tree. But he doesn't stop. He seems to keep knowing where to go. Through the pouring rain he's a ghost, shifting in and out of my vision.

I trip on a rock and look down to regain my footing and when I look up I can't see him. There are blurry shapes everywhere but none of them look like my brother. 'Angus!' I shout. 'Angus?' The sound of water hammering down through all the leaves nearly swallows my voice whole.

'I'm here!' A shout to my left. 'Over here!' An Angus-sized shape waves at me.

He's huddling underneath a big fallen tree and I squeeze in next to him. It's dry underneath the log, but we're both soaked through. 'This is ridiculous,' I say. 'My shoes are buggered.' I wiggle my toes and water squelches out from the seams.

'It's going to be *so* amazing,' says Angus. 'We're close. I know we're close.'

'No,' I say. 'This is insane. We should go back. Do you even know where we are?'

He's not listening. He says, 'I can't wait to see their faces. I'm gonna be like, *read it and weep.* They're go—'

There's a flash of lightning and for an instant the whole world lights up and my eye lands on a dark shape on the ridge below us, moving slightly but noticeably, like a muscle tensing. I blink and the world turns back to grey sheets of rain.

'What was—' I start talking but Angus cuts me off.

'That was it!' he shouts. He grabs my arm. 'Clancy, that was it! You saw it too! Right?'

'I saw—'

'The motherfucking beast!' Angus scrambles to his feet. 'We gotta go.' He charges off into the rain, disappearing as if slipping through the gap in a curtain. Then there's a crash of leaves and a branch tearing and he yells out.

I run towards the sound but immediately slip on the ground and hit a rock, landing right on my backbone and the pain jars me all the way up to my skull. I roll over and a sharp rock gets me in the ribs and it hurts like hell but I shout out, 'Angus!' and there's his yell again and it sounds ages away. I get up and move forward even though it's like someone's stabbing me right beside my kidneys and my vision's doubling up. I'm about to take another step when there's another lightning flash and I see I'm standing at the edge of a cliff and the strap of Angus's backpack is caught on a shrub beside it.

I crouch down and shuffle to the precipice, the rain pounding buckets into my back. I see Angus on a ledge way down below and his leg's twisted up behind him and his face is twisted up too.

*There's no way* down. This is what I keep thinking. There's no way down. I hang one foot off the edge, searching vainly for a foothold. 'Angus!' I shout. 'Are you all right?'

'I'm okay,' he shouts back, but his face tells me he's in pain.

'I can't get down there!'

'Where's the bag?'

'What?'

'Where's the bag?'

I grab the backpack from beside me and hold it over the edge. 'It's here, I've got it!'

Thunder cracks above us and Angus yells out 'Photo! Get the photo!' He's lying there with a broken leg and he still won't give up on the beast.

'You've got to get a shot of it!' he shouts again. 'We've got—AGHFUCK!' He tries to get up and crumples back down.

'I'll get help!' I shout. 'Stay there and I'll get help!' I pull the bag towards me and God bless my ridiculous brother because he's clipped the car keys onto a metal ring that hangs off one of the zips. I search the bag for anything helpful but there's only the camera and a wrinkly apple and another battery and an old porno. A scientist is always prepared, my arse. This was Angus's *survival* kit. But underneath there's something. A fricking *raincoat*. You've got to be kidding me.

I crawl back to the edge and shout, 'Care package!' and drop the bag down and it lands next to him and he scrambles for it. I waggle the keys like *I've got this!* and shout, 'I'll be right back! I'm getting help and I'm coming *right back.*'

Angus shouts something like, 'Okay!' but I can't hear it because of the thunder and I see him waving to me but he can only move one arm and I shout, 'I'll be *right* back!' and I'm thinking, don't die. You absolute dickhead, don't die.

I scramble back up and find the fallen tree. All right, I think. Up the slope. Start with that. I walk slowly but purposefully back up the hill, watching nothing but my feet. My back's caning. I try to remember which way we came from the clearing but my brain scrambles up directions like it always does and I wish to hell that I had a phone. Mum and Dad, so concerned about their family doing things together but they can't even buy their teenage daughter a mobile for emergencies.

In my head the dark shape looms again, lit by the lightning flash. It has to have been a rock or another fallen tree or a trick of our eyes. It has to be. I push the vision from my head and focus on my hopeless boots, full of water, sinking over and over into the leaves and dirt. I reach the top of the slope and plunge on ahead, trying to imagine the path our feet took on the way in. I grab trees and clumps of grass for purchase and everything's tearing and breaking but I manage to move forward. It all looks the same, like I'm stuck in a cartoon and the background's on a loop. But I struggle on and I'm absolutely sopping, feeling twice my weight.

It's then I see the broken tree, the branch twisted over. I'm leaning against it and my breath's all shallow because my back's absolutely killing me and the pain in my ribs has turned weird and fluttery. I walk on and then—thank God—I'm at the clearing. There are huge puddles forming all over the ground, and I think of all Angus's equipment in the hideout. All that bloody money.

The way out is clear enough and somehow I find my way back to the road. The cracking thunder sounds like it's right above me. I get to the ute and fumble around with the keys, dropping them twice in the mud until at last they go in the lock and I can open the door, jump into the driver's seat and finally shut the world out.

The rain hammers on the roof. I take a deep breath and put the keys into the ignition. Not quite how I'd imagined my maiden voyage behind the wheel of a car.

Keep calm, I tell myself. Dozens of diagrams flash in front of me: scores of road rules, correct distances and give way progressions, all thoroughly useless in a thunderstorm in the middle of nowhere with your brother lying at the bottom of a cliff.

*Come on, faggot*, says my brain.

I hit the steering wheel to cut off my thoughts. I put the key into the ignition, turn the key so the engine starts up. A blast of cold air hits me and the radio comes on. I put the car in first gear and go to move forward but it stalls immediately.

*Useless lezzo queer.*

I turn on the lights, and the car's slipped forward off the road so I put it in reverse and try again. The car jerks back, the engine cuts and it rolls further forward. I wrench up the handbrake and the car's sitting there, about to sink into the mud.

*All the Underhills are fucking psycho.*

Okay. I think. One thing at a time. I think back to all the driving questions I pestered Mum and Dad and Angus with. There's no other traffic anywhere on the road. I can do everything one step at a time. Slowly, finally, I get the clutch to bite and I reverse back. I switch the wipers on and am about to drive off when the sight of a nearby tree makes me stop. I get out of the car, stripping off my jumper. I tie it to the tree, pulling the arms as tight as I can to seal the knot.

I get back in the car and drive forward slowly, following

247

the faint grooves Angus's tyres have made in the fire track. Water washes across the track diagonally, shimmering under the headlights. Somehow I don't get bogged and I get to the sealed road and my head's going *left or right?* because somehow I can't even remember which way we came in. I slow the car to a halt and my head's hurting so much and it's only one of two decisions but apparently this is still too much for me.

Left, I decide. Left, and I power up the high-beams and swing the wheel and gun the engine. I peer over the dashboard like an old lady as I drive and all the while I'm thinking of Angus lying on the ledge in the rain with his broken leg and I'm not really sure how I'm supposed to get help because I can hardly see anything in front of me let alone either side so I just keep going.

It feels like forever and my legs start to cramp up from staying tense on the pedals. My eyes are so tired. I have to squint at the tiny stretch of road in front of me and I keep losing focus. I rub my eyes and it feels so good to keep them closed but I know I can't. I force them open and go to yawn but it kills my ribs when I do. And then I can't even breathe in without it hurting so I lose my breath and start coughing and this makes it worse and I actually shiver with pain and something keeps stabbing me in the side and my head's stretching and the road's going blurry and then this light—this whole, all-encompassing light—comes out of nowhere and there's suddenly two legs up ahead and I wrench the wheel left and the car's swerving everywhere and the lights hit swishing grass and my stomach turns over and something cuts me in half and I shout in pain and then it's like hands hitting all up the doors and then something shears through my chest. I keep screaming, not because it helps, but because everything sounds bloated and deep, and I want to cut through it. Everything's going dark and all I can think is *my shoes are so wet, how am I supposed to get around in wet shoes*?

*My mouth's sort* of gummy when I wake up but when I try to turn over to where I usually have a glass of water the entire side of my body stings and when I open my eyes it doesn't seem to be my bedroom. My hand's warm, and I think Titch has put it in a bowl of water so I'll pee myself while I'm sleeping but when I move it I realise it's warm because someone's holding it.

I try to move my fingers but nothing really happens. It's like my thoughts are on the other side of a fogged-up window.

'Hey there,' says Mum's voice. I follow the sound and her face is there. There's a plastic curtain behind her and maybe I'm in the shower? Why would I be in the shower? I concentrate harder and remember our shower curtain is green. This curtain is a patterned blue.

I think I say, 'Hi,' but I'm not really sure this is what's come out of my mouth. All the lines of things are fuzzy and then I can't remember if things are actually *supposed* to have lines around them. I hear music, somewhere.

'How are you feeling?' Mum's pulled her hair back so I can see her freckles. On the window next to the bed there's water running down in racing lines.

And then I remember the rain and the lightning and the cliff and the car and then it's all tumbling back like a dream except in reverse because memories are flooding back from real life instead of my subconscious.

'Angus,' I say. 'He's on the thing.' I try to lift my head but I'm already too dizzy from talking. 'He's got the back-pack, but he's fallen off.' There's the image of my brother's face, twisted up, spattered with mud.

Mum squeezes my hand again. 'Angus is okay,' she says. 'He's here as well. He's fine.'

*Here?* I think. Here. Then I roll my eyes, like *der, Fred.* Hospital. I'm in hospital. 'What happened? How long...'

'You had an accident,' Mum says. 'You were driving.'

She talks like she's not even mad, which doesn't make sense. I *was* driving. No, I crashed the car. I remember. My first time behind the wheel and I crash the car. 'Is Angus's ute okay? I didn't mean to.'

'Don't worry about it, Clancy. For goodness sake. You were so lucky. You were both so lucky.'

'Did I wreck it?'

'There was a road crew. They were there, otherwise...' Mum wipes her eyes with a tissue.

There's the set of legs rushing up towards me on the road, a jolt in my shoulders as I wrench the wheel. 'I

251

swerved. They were in my way. I could hardly even see.'

'You went off the road. They said the car rolled. In a field. You were so lucky.'

Yeah, I think. Lucky: I get it. My mind's trying to ratchet further back—something else I have to remember—but nothing will catch. 'Angus is okay?' Then, 'Did he get out? How did he get out?'

'You really...You told them, Clancy. You told them where he was, how to get to him.'

'I did?' I can't remember this at all, which is probably why I gave them the right directions.

Mum nods. 'They said you'd tied your jumper to a tree. So clever. They found the tent, and you'd broken branches so they could find the way.'

The jumper. Time's jumping backwards. Had I broken the branches? I say, 'A good scientist is always prepared.' Then I cough, and my chest explodes in pain. And it's like this has jump-started all my nerve endings because the rest of me starts to hurt, too. 'Aaah. What's going on in there?' I rub my side, where the worst of the pain is blaring out from.

Mum guides my hand back to hers. 'You cracked some ribs,' she says, 'among other things. You bruised your coccyx.'

'My coccyx?' Jesus, even when I hurt myself it has to be the most embarrassing-sounding place. 'What about Angus?'

'He's broken his leg and some other bones, got some

cuts and bruises. He's still under sedation, but they say he'll be fine.' All the while, Mum hasn't even sounded angry or asked why we were messing around on clifftops in the middle of nowhere.

'Is Dad here?' I say.

'He's taking a little walk,' she says. 'Titch doesn't really like hospitals.'

'Poor Titch.' The little bastard was probably guilting Dad into guiding him on a healing journey to a vending machine. Titch hates not only hospitals but anything that doesn't feature the phrase *flavour explosion*.

'Reeve was here too. Earlier.'

'Reeve? Reeve's here?'

'He was who called us. Last night. He was at the hospital. He found out everything he could and stayed so he could fill us in.'

'He called you? What? Why?'

'They found his phone number in your pocket. It was all you had on you.' Mum reaches over me to the bedside table. Reeve's business card, crumpled and smeared with mud. *Reeve Lewis: Senior Executive Retail Law Enforcement Officer, Esq.*

I smile. Thank Christ I never clean out my pockets. If I hadn't—

And then I remember Sasha. And running from the house. Leaving Nancy. The car. Macca's. The observatory. The kiss. No, no, no. And then, impossibly fast, the rest of it falls into place. All my fuzzy thoughts finally snap into focus and I remember all of it. I kissed her. It happened. It really did. I try to shrink back into the bed, to disappear. If only I could slip back into unconsciousness. There's no responsibility there. Where's the machine that turns up the painkillers?

I must make a noise because Mum goes, 'Are you okay? I can get a nurse if it's the pain.'

I shake my head.

'What is it?'

I can't tell her. Oh God. The biggest mistake of my life. One hundred per cent *real*. A wave of exhaustion comes over me, and I realise my jaw is clenched shut. I try to relax it, but I can't work out how. I stretch my eyes wide. My skin feels so heavy, like it's sinking down through the pillow. 'I'm sorry, Mum,' I hear myself say.

'Nothing to be sorry for, sweetie. I'm just glad you're safe.'

'No,' I say. 'Not about Angus or whatever. I left you all behind. I abandoned you.'

'Don't try to say too much. You probably just need rest.'

'I got all...' the words just aren't there. 'I got all *tangled* up.'

'Tangled up?'

'Everything's gone wrong. I got everything wrong. I thought Sasha liked me.'

'Who's Sasha?'

There's an echo in the room. This makes no sense.

Everyone knows who Sasha is. Everyone knew Sasha. 'She's got the car, but it's not hers.' I close my eyes. 'She's going to be a model and she invited me. And I tried to kiss her and then I was going to…off the tower. But it wasn't water.'

'Maybe just let yourself rest,' says Mum's voice.

'I loved her,' my voice says. 'We were going to live in a cabin and eat dinner. We'd eat late.' My thoughts are getting spongy.

Mum squeezes me hand again, but it feels like my arm's at the end of a really long road. 'Ask Dad when the cricket starts,' I say.

'Okay, sweetie.'

'I love you Mum. I love everybody.' I'm nearly at the bottom of a comfy dark swimming pool. 'I just wish I knew what the hell I was doing.'

*I wake up* at what appears to be the right time for a nurse to bring me breakfast. I sort of nod at her and she leaves me with a teabag steeping in lukewarm water, a tiny orange juice and travel pack of Special K. I never get Coco Pops. This reminds me of Nancy. Just another victim of my recent scorched-earth social policy. Another casualty of my misplaced loyalty.

Everything was fine up until Dad's accident. I was getting by fine on my own. Maybe I could again. Except I'll never be allowed to. By the time school starts, everyone in Barwen will know about Sasha and me. They probably already do.

There's no way I can go back to the Beauty Station. One Raylene McCarthy I can handle, but it won't stop with just her. Buggs's family and the rest of the Barwen royalty will be out in force. Eloise doesn't deserve that, having to ruin her business to keep me on. The only thing worse than employing a murderer's daughter would be employing a murderer's gay daughter.

All these thoughts are with me constantly. Probably I should be enjoying the isolation of a hospital bed. Perhaps I should be absorbing every overacted moment of the silent soap opera playing on the TV bolted to the wall. Maybe I should appreciate the lack of input from the old woman lying on the bed next to me, snoring through her open mouth. I should be lapping up these moments of anonymity, while my identity is still just a tick or a cross on a doctor's clipboard.

A rustling noise shocks me, and I look up to see Reeve in the doorway with a bunch of cellophane-wrapped flowers so crazily colourful they can't possibly be real.

'Oh hey,' I say. 'How's it going?'

'How are *you* going, more like.'

'Been better, I guess.'

'They said you were awake, so…Does it hurt? You broke your rib?'

'Three of them, apparently. It's not so bad. I'm riding on a fluffy morphine cloud most of the time, anyway.'

Reeve goes, 'Always with the morphine,' with a perfectly executed Dr Hibbert chuckle.

I smile. It's weird to see him. My thoughts are still a little muddled, but isn't he supposed to hate me? 'Hey thanks,' I say. 'I really owe you.'

He waves a hand, like *forget about it*. 'Probably the first and last time someone's going to use one of my business cards.'

'Your business cards save lives.'

Reeve puts the flowers down on the end of the bed, eyeing the bouquet uncomfortably the way most boys do: *I've given you these and now they're yours and you can figure out what to do with them.*

'Sit down,' I say. 'You'll only catch a minor disease from the chair, probably.'

He says, 'I'm just glad you're okay. That you're both okay.'

'Thanks for the flowers. You didn't have to bring them.'

Reeve shrugs. 'You have to bring *something*, don't you. For some reason I had it in my head that you were supposed to bring grapes to people in hospital, but I don't know if you like them.'

'Flamin' botoxed sultanas,' I say, recycling a joke from months ago, a slow day at the shopping centre when we tried to think up insults for every item in the fruit shop.

Reeve laughs, finally sitting down. 'This was the second-cheapest bouquet they had at the florist,' he says, patting the cellophane. 'I hope you appreciate that.'

'You know how to make a woman feel special,' I say, trying to flutter my eyelids and probably not succeeding. Reeve's face goes red. I'm an idiot.

'Listen,' I say. 'Really. Thanks. For everything. I mean, I'm not the easiest person to get along with.'

'Yes you are.' He's got the look of someone who's

trying to remember an obscure address.

'No. I'm not. I ran off in the middle of lunch, for one thing.'

'Well, that's—I mean, it didn't worry me. Why, um, did you though?'

This is a good question. 'I thought it was…something I had to do. I thought it was important.'

'And was it?'

'Not really. I thought it was. But it really wasn't.'

'Oh well,' he says. 'Good that you know now, hey?'

'Was everyone pissed off?'

'Not pissed off. Not really. Your mum and dad seemed…embarrassed, I guess, more than anything.'

I cringe. 'Yeah, I'll bet. It was supposed to be this big *together* thing for the family. I put paid to that.' Then, 'What about Nancy? Was she okay?'

'I think so. I mean, her mum sort of made them leave. The whole thing wrapped up pretty quickly.'

'Oh, God.' Carla would definitely not want Nancy being around me now.

'No, it was fine,' Reeve says. 'I just hung out with Angus and then got to take basically the whole lasagne home with me. It was amazing.'

'You had to talk to Angus? Sorry.'

'Nah, he's cool. I never really hung out with him at school but he's okay.'

'My *brother* Angus? I'm sure there's a head trauma specialist you could see while you're here.'

Reeve laughs. 'He's got some interesting ideas, I'll give you that. But he's a good guy.'

I picture—again—the image of the dirt below the observatory, looming up towards me. I feel Angus's grip on my arm, refusing to let me go. 'Yeah,' I say. 'He actually might be.'

'Up on the mountain,' says Reeve. 'That was something to do with Angus, wasn't it? That's why you were up there. Before lunch he was going on about this *amazing discovery* he was about to make. Wouldn't say what it was.'

There's the other image I can't shake: the black shape I saw in the lightning; the giant, moving muscle.

'Just one of his schemes,' I say. 'One of many.' For some reason, I want to protect my brother. I want his secret kept. 'He owes you one as well.'

Reeve shakes his head, like *nah*. 'You're the hero of this one, Clance. You're the one who drove back down the mountain. I knew you were keen to get your licence, but man...'

'They'll never let me drive now. I left the ute upside-down in a field.'

'No,' he says. 'It was really...a really brave thing to do. Really brave.'

A fresh wave of exhaustion hits me. 'Why is everyone being so nice to me?'

'What do you mean?'

I feel tears welling up. 'I mean, everyone's acting like

I'm this amazing person, but I'm just a weird freak. A crazy weird freak.'

'No you're not,' says Reeve. 'You're the best person I know.' He takes my hand, quickly, but his big hands are warm. His mouth is crushed up, like he doesn't know what expression to make.

'I'm always going to disappoint you. I disappoint everyone.'

'Why?' His thumb moves gently over the back of my hand.

'Because I can't...I can't be who you want me to be.' My words are a loosened knot.

'You don't have to be anyone.'

I stare at the bridge of his nose. 'I can't be...someone who's with you. Is what I'm saying.'

His thumb stops moving. He takes his hand away.

'It's not you, though,' I say. 'It's not because it's you. It's anyone. Any boy...man. That's not who I am. I really like you but I can't...like you the way you want me to.' My thoughts are in a spiral and I have no way of knowing if he understands.

Reeve's quiet for a moment. Then he nods. 'I see,' he says. 'I mean, I understand.'

I'm not ready to tell him. I just can't. 'You're too nice,' I say. 'You deserve so much happiness, or wealth, or pancakes. A girl who can make you happier than I can.'

He says, quietly, 'We all need people who make us feel like ourselves.'

The big, beautiful idiot is making me cry. I've got new tears welling up behind tears and more just behind. Like an army assembling. Like shark's teeth. 'Why are you so nice?' I say.

'Don't worry,' he says. 'I'm awful to you behind your back.'

I laugh. 'You're going to make beautiful nerdy babies with someone one day, Reeve. And that someone will be the luckiest person.'

He smiles. It's killing him, I know, but he smiles.

Angus is discharged from hospital and I'm not allowed to leave with him. This strikes me as grossly unfair, since he fell off a cliff and I just fell over. Turns out I did the most damage slipping over in the rain, then the car crash endangered a random selection of internal organs. Angus just had *clean breaks* and *simple bruising* and other annoyingly straightforward injuries. One of my ribs came close to puncturing my lung, so I had to stay longer *for observation*. Somehow, the thought of being observed seems worse than anything my own body could do to me.

In the afternoons I'm sometimes allowed to come down to what the hospital laughingly calls a garden, which is really just a pot-planted segment of negative space between two buildings. It's not outside, exactly, because it's walled in, but in the afternoon a wafer of light and some fresh air sneak through the louvres.

I'm there in my wheelchair on the Sunday before

school's supposed to start, reading a compellingly bad romance novel, when I realise someone is standing behind me.

'Mum didn't really want me to come,' is the first thing I hear Nancy say. She walks around in front of me. She's wearing her sunglasses, even though it's not at all bright.

All I can come up with is, 'Okay.'

I try to stuff the book down the side of my chair. The nurse brought around a literal crate of books once I was able to sit up in bed and they were all Mills and Boon. Cheesy and embarrassing tales of initially doomed but eventually hunky-dory boy/girl love. Reading them is like sculling raspberry cough syrup.

Nancy just stands there, and we're both not saying anything, and it's like our friendship is back to square one.

'So,' I say. 'Listen.' I drag a blanket across my bare legs. I haven't seen myself in a mirror for a long time but I can imagine how I look. 'Thanks for coming.' Is this it? Is this the best I can come up with?

Nancy shrugs. 'I brought you a card. It's from everyone at Nature Club. They were all going to come, but I thought you wouldn't like that very much.' She hands me an envelope. It's homemade paper, pressed with leaves. Everyone's written inside, with predictably insane handwriting except for Olive and Tom's exact cursive. There's no message from Nancy.

'The paper's nice,' I say. 'Did you make it?'

'No.'

'Well, it's nice.'

'Uh-huh.'

This is going to go on forever. 'I'm sorry I was a dick.'

Nancy goes, 'Which particular time?' which is a fair point.

'The most recent time,' I say. 'And the other times. And any future times.'

'Right from the heart, then.' Nancy starts grinding her teeth. I can see the muscles in her jaw moving.

Bloody hell. 'I really am sorry,' I say. 'I just—I feel like all I do in my life is apologise to people.'

'Maybe there's a reason for that.'

I take a few deep breaths. 'Why did you even come,' I say, 'if you didn't want to be here? If your mum didn't want you to come, why bother?'

'I thought we were friends,' she says. Her voice drops. 'I thought I'd found a friend.'

'But I thought—'

'You told me all that stuff about you. Personal stuff. And then you just disappeared. You went off in some stranger's car and I was so confused and no one knew what was going on and...then you were in this car crash.' She clamps her hand over her mouth like she's stifling a sudden violent yawn. 'I had to find out from the newspaper.'

'How was the crossword?'

'Shut up, Clancy!' She glares at me. 'Not everything's a...goddamn joke. You nearly died.'

'Sorry.' I am truly the worst. 'I don't know why...' But

I know exactly why. Stupid jokes mean I don't have to think about the image of the smashed sunglasses or the Beast of Barwen or Sasha's face as she pulled away from me.

'Forget it,' says Nancy. 'Enjoy the card. Enjoy your life.' She walks past me.

I ram my wheelchair backwards, blocking the door.

'Please move,' she says.

I say, as quickly as I can, 'It was the girl. In the car. The girl I told you about.'

Nancy squints at me. 'The girl?'

'The girl I like. Sasha. We'd organised a...we were going to hang out. But not then. She wasn't supposed to show up then.'

'Oh.' Nancy takes off her sunglasses. I can see she's been crying.

'I was...I thought she liked me. She didn't, though. She really didn't. That's why. That's why I left. It was so stupid.'

Nancy's face fills with confusion. 'You should have told me.'

'I didn't know she was going to show up. I didn't think.'

'And you'd walk out on your family as well. Without telling anyone. People don't do that. You can't just leave.'

There's something in her eyes, behind the brimming tears. I recognise the familiar rage of white-hot embarrassment. 'Are you okay?' I say. 'Why don't you sit down?' There's a bench by the other wall that people only ever use

266

to stand next to and smoke.

Nancy says, 'I should probably just go, I think. I hope you feel better. She pushes her sunglasses down and goes to move past me.

I move my wheelchair back further. 'You're not leaving,' I say.

'Get. Out. Of. My. Way.'

'Just five minutes. Please.'

She stares at me.

'If you want to leave,' I say, 'you'll have to knock over an injured girl in a wheelchair. Do you want that on your conscience?'

She sighs. She walks over to the bench and sits down, pulling her legs up underneath her.

I take my time. I tell Nancy the whole sorry story properly. No confusion. No dancing around the issue. This is who I am and this is what I did. I tell it properly. Me, Sasha, the skate park, the roadhouse, the hideout, the date, the observatory, the kiss. Buggs, the car, the graffiti. It feels horrible to relive my humiliation, but maybe telling it to someone makes it slightly better. Sunlight weakens and the afternoon lingers.

All throughout, Nancy just stares at the ground. 'This is like what happened before,' she says eventually. 'At my old school. I trusted someone. This girl in my grade. I thought we were really close.' She scrunches up her face. 'My dad,' she says. 'He's not overseas. Or, well, he might be. I don't know.'

267

I grab her hand without thinking. Squeeze it.

'He left a few years ago. Didn't really give a reason, at least not one that Mum told me. It was so awful.'

'I'm really sorry,' I say.

'Yeah, well...I started feeling really bad. *Really* bad. Just awful, dark thoughts. I told this girl—my so-called friend—about it. I didn't know who else to talk to. Then the next week everyone's looking at me like I'm on fire. Drawing red lines on their wrists. Pretending to choke. Making jokes in chemistry about keeping the acid away from me. Just sneaky, awful things the teachers wouldn't notice.'

'Bloody hell.' And then, 'If I'd known...'

'It's fine,' she says through a stream of tears. 'It is. I just really need people to like me, apparently.' She laughs, even though it isn't at all funny.

'It's screwed up,' I say, 'isn't it? When you need to talk to people but you can't talk to people. Like, if we'd told each other this stuff earlier...'

'Neither of us would've though.'

'True.'

Nancy leans forward and puts her head in her hands. I stroke her back. Just two broken peas in a pod.

'When are you coming back to school?' says Nancy, eventually, from behind her hair.

'They think I'll be out some time next week. Not exactly looking forward to going back, but Mum'll kill me if I don't.'

'So will I. I'll have to sit with Glenn at lunch.'

'Dear God.'

'He's fine. He's harmless. But I'm in serious danger of becoming interested in World of Warcraft.'

'It can't be any worse than this world. Man, the shit I'm going to cop for the Sasha stuff...'

Nancy sits up. 'Do you think it'll be that bad?'

I give her a look like *Really?* 'She'll probably say I attacked her or tricked her or something. She'll want to turn the story her way.'

'Yeah,' says Nancy, slumping her shoulders. 'That sounds about right.'

I go, 'I just don't understand her deal. She didn't... When I started to kiss her. She kind of started too...'

'Yeah, well I know what my counsellor would say. *She's working through her own issues. You just happened to be in the wrong place at the wrong time.* Which is probably right, but it doesn't make it any less shit for you.'

'Yeah.' I roll my wheelchair back and forth. 'She seemed like this...doorway. Like, the answer to all my problems.'

'We live and learn,' Nancy says. 'Well, we *live*, anyway. Mostly.'

I stretch. 'I'm just looking forward to getting back to my own bed, at the very least.'

'Do your family know? About...?'

I groan. 'I don't know. Maybe. I think I might have told Mum when I was still drugged up. I hope not.'

269

'It might help. Telling them. It might make things easier.'

I bite the inside of my cheek. 'The old emotional contract, hey?'

Nancy smiles. 'Stupid name, I guess. But the idea's not all bad.'

'Well,' I say. 'Maybe.'

'Whatever happens, at school,' she says, 'I've got your back.'

'Thanks. So you're staying then? In Barwen?'

'Yeah, of course. They finally sorted the house out. No more motel. No more Danny's Ristorant.'

'That's so great,' I say, as a little ballast is cut free from my mind. 'So great.' Somewhere above us, a generator clanks on. The day's disappearing. 'So we should start work on that friendship manual,' I say.

'Hah! Yeah. Don't want anyone else ending up like us.'

'Don't want *us* ending up like us.'

Nancy smiles. 'I don't know about that. I think we're worth the few extra chapters.'

She's got this long dress on that shimmers, even under the vapid blare of the shopping centre's fluorescent lights.

'Are you going to an awards show after work?' I say.

'Every day is a reward, my darling,' says Eloise. 'Never forget this. And it never harms to add a little glamour to life!' She dips her shoulder like in a tango and despite myself I laugh. 'But it is so wonderful to see you, Clancy!' She leans over the counter to kiss me on both cheeks.

It feels weird to be standing outside the booth. Everything seems nothing like it's supposed to.

'Just one moment, per favore,' Eloise says to Mrs Capshaw—one of a gaggle of pensioners she gives free makeovers to in exchange for their loyalty—who is sitting on one of the stools by the Hollywood mirror.

Mrs Capshaw nods, gives me a little wave. 'Good to see you back love.'

I wave back, a nervous smile bouncing onto my face.

It's my first trip to town since coming out of hospital. I had to literally wrench myself free of Mum's grasp when she dropped me off.

It's great to be back home, but it's still driving me crazy. Angus and I are both recovering, which means, basically, me trying to use the TV to rewatch all of *Gilmore Girls* and my brother violently disagreeing. I needed to see the outside world, at least once, before I have to go back to school next week.

'How are you, my darling?' Eloise holds one hand to my cheek, searching me out with her opal eyes.

'I'm fine,' I say, trying to muster as much positivity as I can. 'You know…' I try to indicate my entire body. The worst of it is I have no injuries you can see. Not like Angus, who's been using his cast and crutches as a universal get-out-of-responsibility-free card.

'So brave,' Eloise says. 'Everyone knows how brave you are, now. For all things.'

I furrow my brow. I'm not sure I want to go into the full extent of my supposed bravery. Anyway, so far this morning no one has shouted at me, called me names or done any of the horrible things my brain has been imagining.

The day is still young, of course.

I smell cinnamon and hot oil behind me. 'What's the nine-oh-seven?' I say, even before turning around.

Reeve looks shocked. 'I was going to surprise you.'

'Need to work on your ninja skills,' I say. I yoink a donut from his bag.

Reeve lowers his voice. 'So listen, I thought you'd want to know.' He stops there.

I stare at him. 'Want to know what?'

'About the accident.'

'Which one?'

He winces. 'Sorry. The one your dad was involved in.'

My heartbeat jerks. 'What about it?'

'Charlie Jencke. They finally...' he lowers his voice again. 'They did the autopsy.'

I pull the donut away from my face. 'Right. And?'

'He'd been drinking. They found alcohol in his system, and weed.'

'Shit. How do you know?'

'I have my sources.' He takes a big bite and there's cinnamon on his top lip. 'Tran at the print shop,' he says with his mouth full. 'His brother works at the medical centre. But guess what?'

I give him a stare like *just tell me*.

'The booze was one thing, but the real thing is the car had something wrong with it. The wheel alignment or something. Would've affected how it braked.'

'So...it was the car?'

Reeve shrugs. 'Don't know for sure. But guess who sold his dad the car? Guess who serviced it?'

Everything goes slow as I try to catch up to Reeve's words.

'Pfister. Motors.' He punctuates each word with a finger. 'And guess which Pfister was supposed to have done the roadworthy? Our friend Buggs.'

'Holy shit.'

'The police are looking at the whole set-up.'

'But Buggs's uncle is a cop.'

'That's what makes it so good! It's this big thing, now. This whole investigation.'

'God. What about Dad?'

'I dunno, but I'm pretty sure in a couple of days the Pfisters are all the town's going to be talking about.'

I look around me, at all the people walking past, going about their lives. Families with trolleys, a trail of kids behind. Old guys with flannel shirts and a farmer's stoop. A group of girls, younger than me, in matching cut-offs and singlets, vamping to their own internal top-forty soundtracks. Are they worrying about anyone else but themselves? Are they thinking about me, or Dad, or Charlie Jencke, or Buggs or Sasha?

'It's good news,' says Reeve. 'It'll take all the heat off your dad.'

'I guess.' I suppose it should make me happy, but all I can think about is Charlie's family, and Cassandra's. Whoever they get to blame, it won't change what happened.

I watch Mrs Capshaw tottering past me, top heavy with makeup, and I wave.

'You are not too distracted from your job, Security Guard Lewis?' Eloise taps the side of her head with the end of a makeup brush.

'Just filling Clancy in on the latest retail strategies,' Reeve says.

'Well, she probably has plenty of other things on her mind than that.'

Reeve gives me eyes like *that's my cue* and hands me the bag with the last donut in it. 'Coffee,' he says, 'next week? Maybe?'

'Definitely,' I say.

We're on the verandah squeezing the last moments from Sunday. Angus is having beers and I've had half of one because he can't open the bottles with his arm in a cast, which is pretty great. Titch has got the hose on. He's made a river around his feet that runs back under the house and probably pools around my broken bike. It's still under there somewhere but I'm hoping I won't get a new one. I'm hoping a car is the next step. No one's realised Angus's bike is missing, or at least no one's mentioned it to me. I guess wrecking his ute was a masterstroke of diversion.

Dad's coming up the driveway and, as he steps from the car, he's still got his towel wrapped around him from the pool. I wish we had a pool. It's like the rain's still in the ground and the sun's pulling it out, making it slap us in the face as it floats back to the clouds. I pull a flannel out of the esky that holds the beer and the ice pack for my ribs and drape it back over my face.

'Did you bring ice-creams?' says Titch, whose concept of a pool doesn't proceed past the refreshment stand.

'Clancy would like a Gaytime,' says Angus, and I take the flannel off and fake-punch his cast so he flinches like a baby.

'How was aquarobics, Dad?' I say.

'Pretty good,' he says. 'Still the youngest person there.' He stretches from side to side, doing fake swimming moves that would have had him white with pain a few weeks ago.

'Yeah,' I say, 'but only by a fortnight or so.'

'Cheeky bugger,' says Dad. He takes off his towel—thankfully he's wearing boardies underneath—and twirls it around into a point.

'Perfect,' he says. 'Still wet enough to have a bit of weight behind it.'

'I'm injured,' I say. 'You can't towel-flick an injured girl.'

'Yeah,' says Angus. 'She might fall over and break her butt again.'

I stand up and shove my arse in his face. 'You can suck my coccyx.'

Dad raises his hands. 'I'll leave you two great minds alone. Dinner at six-thirty.'

Angus and I give him a salute as he disappears inside.

'Get us another beer, can you?' says Angus.

I go, 'Mate, Fair Go At Work!' and he cracks up.

Some lady came down from Brisbane once the accident report came out, turned up on our doorstep in this

277

polo shirt with *Fair Go at Work!* on the front and back. Angus and I kept saying it to each other until Mum made us stop.

That night, Dad told us she was with the State Government and they wanted to talk to him about the council's treatment of workers. She went over the accident with him, but also his back injury and how he'd got bugger-all support. The night of the crash he'd gone nine hours without a break. He's already got some backdated compo, with maybe more to come.

Angus burps loudly. 'Looking forward to school tomorrow?'

I make a foghorn noise. 'Don't remind me. Might still get out of it. I mean, come on.' I lift up my shirt where the yellow bruise still shows the outline of my ribs.

'Put 'em away. Jesus.'

I stretch my side, testing the dull ache for the millionth time.

'Gotta face it sometime,' he says. 'Gotta get those good grades.'

'God.' I rake my hands over my face. 'Gotta face my new identity, you mean.'

'New identity?'

'I'm a gay weirdo now, not just a regular weirdo. Sasha's made sure of that.'

'Nah.' Angus takes a sip of beer. 'She's finished now, all that shit with Buggs and his dad, that's all anyone cares about. Bloody classic.'

I put my feet up on the esky. 'I dunno. Mum wants me to talk to a counsellor.'

'Get you scared straight?'

'Piss off. No, just generally.'

'Might help. Never know.' He finishes his beer. 'The Gaytime stuff. You know I'm just giving you shit?'

'It's all going in my tell-all autobiography,' I say, 'all the hate crimes. You'll get yours at the Hague.'

Angus laughs. 'I did save your life.'

'I did save yours.'

'True.'

I wiggle lower in my chair, stretching my feet out to catch the last of the sun's warmth.

'What about you?' I say. 'What's the next great expedition?'

'Eh. Get a job, I guess. There's a vacancy at the Beauty Station, isn't there?'

'Only until final term's over. Gonna sell so much Beauty over the holidays.'

Angus sighs. 'Gonna write to the manufacturer of that tripod,' he says, for the thousandth time. His camera and sound recorder were wrecked when a branch came down on the hideout, tearing a hole in the tent, letting the water in. 'If it hadn't fallen over, we would've had the footage. I wouldn't have ended up breaking my bloody arm. I could've had real evidence.' He stares at his cast. 'I dunno.'

We haven't really talked about that night on the

mountain, about the dark shape lit by lightning. Perhaps it was something, perhaps it was nothing. Perhaps it doesn't matter.

I go, 'You still heading to the mines?'

'Maybe. Got no savings now. Might get some work in town. Maybe stack shelves for a bit.'

'You could go back to uni.'

'Yeah, maybe. If I wait a year I can move out with you.'

'No. Way.'

'Come on, it'll be great! I'll show you the ways of the world.'

'I should've left you at the bottom of that cliff.'

'Then you wouldn't have been able to wreck my car.'

Angus raises his empty bottle and I bump it with my fist.

'To the future,' he says.

'To the future,' I say. 'And whatever's after that.'

# ACKNOWLEDGMENTS

This book was a strange convergence of luck, timing and people being very patient with me, so I would like to sincerely thank:

My wonderful family, especially my parents Paul and Judy and my brother Andrew, for always being there for me (and in the case of my brother, lending me money and a laptop right when I needed it most).

My incomparable editor Mandy Brett, who acted not at all surprised when I brought her a YA book instead of the two other serious adult books I had promised her. Her guidance and advice were, as ever, invaluable.

The early readers of the book, for their encouragement and advice: Leesa Currie, Hannah Andrews, Rebecca Shaw and Judy Currie.

The whole team at Text Publishing, who, as a company, actually stop to have a drink with you when you visit them, and are so supportive it hurts. A special thanks must go to Imogen Stubbs for her amazing cover design. I want to be buried with that font.

My amazing and talented workmates at Avid Reader Bookshop and Where the Wild Things Are, especially my bosses Fiona Stager and Kevin Guy, who show, by example, what pride in your work can really achieve.

The Eleanor Dark Foundation and all at Varuna, the Writers House, as well as the Marten Bequest Travelling Scholarships for allowing me the time and space to write the first and second drafts of Clancy.

My wife and best friend, Leesa, who quit her job to follow me halfway around the world so I could sit and write in a small German village. My darling, you continue to amaze me with your intelligence, your humour, your beauty, and your ongoing willingness to remain married to me.

And finally, I'd like to thank you, the reader, for picking up this book. If it helps just one person understand that being young is being confused, and that things do get better, and that none of us really knows what we're doing, then this whole process will have been worth it. Also, by reading this final sentence you are now legally obliged to buy the book for five of your friends.